CLAIMED

NIGHTWIND PACK

LAURANN DOHNER AN~ ~~~~ ~~~

Kidnapped then released deep in the woods, Brandi is on a harrowing run for her life, hunted by beasts straight out of a horror movie. But there's an even bigger, more vicious creature in the woods — the deadly werewolf who saves her life. Jason is much more than a man, dangerous and intimidating, and Brandi still finds herself wanting every unbelievably sexy inch of him.

When he investigates the desperate screams near his secluded cabin, Jason's shocked to find his own kind hunting a human — but he ends up even more stunned when he accidentally triggers a mating heat in the beautifully lush woman he saved. Overwhelmed with lust, Jason takes her, bites her, binds her to him forever…

Now he just has to break the news to Brandi.

A NOTE FROM THE AUTHORS

Six years ago Kele and Laurann began emailing each other. We became friends and critique partners. That bond grew deeper until we were besties. Both of us have wanted to do a project together but the timing was always off. We'd plot and plan together, having countless conversations, hoping for that day, and then it finally came. The stars aligned, the time was right (LOL), and the Nightwind series came to be. This is the first book in the series and more are coming soon.

ENJOY!

SPECIAL THANKS TO

Kelli Collins for being an amazing editor we both adore.

Dar Albert for the beautiful cover.

Wanda Prezeau for being the best proof reader two authors could hope for.

And most especially, our husbands, for never once complaining about the hours and hours of phone calls we made to each other that were totally essential to writing this book. No, seriously, they were. We swear. They were all 100% business related. ::shifty eyes::

Editor: Kelli Collins
Cover Artist: Dar Albert
ISBN: 978-1-944526-68-9

Chapter One

Brandi wished she could rewind back to this morning and start over. She would have done anything to change the past few hours, but wishing wasn't going to save her life…or her sanity.

Instead she kept running, even though her side hurt and her lungs burned. She dodged a tree and nearly tripped on a root. She stumbled, twisting her ankle, but managed to keep going. The fear was so all-consuming she barely noticed the pain.

She'd die faster if she would just give in, but she didn't want to check out on life. The chilling sound of pounding feet came from behind, closing the distance. Terror flooded her. If she wasn't so out of breath, the scream wanting to rise might have come out. As it was, only a soft moan pushed past her lips.

They could have taken her down by now. She knew they were faster, but they were toying with her, and that made it so much worse. What kind of twisted games were they going to play with her once they caught her?

Her aching muscles, the pain in her side, and the constant struggle to push breath in and out of her lungs that were burning from overuse were making it hard to keep going even in the name of survival. So Brandi's mind roamed to keep her attention off her exhausted body.

****

She'd woken up at five and put her bag inside her car. The drive she'd planned was supposed to take five hours. Her best friend, Jenny, had invited her to spend the weekend. They were going to catch up, do some shopping, and just enjoy each other's company.

Things had gone bad when Brandi pulled over for gasoline in the town of Dryer. It had been the wrong damn place to stop.

She'd been filling her tank at the small, lonely gas station when a van had pulled in behind her to use another pump. She glanced at the other vehicle and the two men inside with passing curiosity. Then she'd ignored them when she saw the men looking back.

She was closing her tank cover when a pair of arms wrapped around her.

Brandi screamed and kicked but the man holding her had been too strong. He easily lifted her off her feet, carrying her to the open side door of the white cargo van in seconds. She landed hard on a metal floor when he threw her inside and the sliding door slammed shut. Brandi was stunned for several breathless moments, but when she did get her bearings, she started screaming again. Even as she tried to find a way to get out, she made noise, hoping someone passing by would hear her.

Willing to leap from a moving vehicle, she wanted out, but the back doors wouldn't open and neither would the side one.

There was a cage-like wall between the back of the van and the front. The man who grabbed her had climbed into the passenger seat. She tried to remember details about him, hoping she'd live long enough to identify him to the police. He was in his late twenties, had short brown hair, and a scar ran across his chin. He had turned and peered at her through the cage, grinning with thin lips when they first pulled out of the gas station. His eyes appeared hauntingly cold. He gave her a lecherous look, staring at her as if she was a trophy, and somehow she could sense the promise of pain and horror in her future. That had been what first forced the screams out of her—the raw terror that one look caused.

The men in front ignored her loud, terrified cries. She threw herself against the back doors, hoping to jar them loose, even if it meant tumbling onto the asphalt. She tried the handles again. She fought with the side door and she didn't once stop shrieking. The driver never turned his head as he pulled off the highway, away from the small town, and into the woods. Brandi's fear escalated as she saw the trees getting denser, knowing there was no one to hear her now.

She stopped screaming. Her throat felt raw and dry. She coughed from the strain. Shaking, she huddled in the back corner of the van praying for a miracle. Someone had to have seen her abduction. Her car remained at the pump, her purse on the driver's seat with the door open, from when she'd put her ATM card away after paying for the gas. The keys were in the ignition.

Hoping, praying, begging for salvation, she listened for police sirens, but no sound came—just the deafening silence of impending doom that echoed like the hard, thumping rhythm of her heartbeat.

Then the van stopped, and Brandi thought she might actually throw up from the mind-numbing terror. All kinds of horrible possibilities had been running through her mind and she wanted to stop all of this before it became a reality, but she was trapped and powerless.

She watched with dread as both men climbed out of the front of the van. She stood up, instantly on the defense. She wasn't going to let them rape her without a battle. She'd seen their faces — and they knew it. She could identify them if she survived whatever other crimes they were about to commit on her. These men weren't going to let her live, but she'd die fighting.

The side door opened and Brandi shouted, utilizing the element of surprise to attack her kidnapper. By using the higher platform of the van to her advantage, she pulled off a short run-tackle that would have made her older football-playing brother proud.

Shock lit up the man's features as her body slammed into his.

The crash to the ground was bone-jarring and he grunted from the impact when Brandi landed on top of him. She went for his eyes with her fingernails. She clawed viciously, feeling a keen sense of satisfaction when he screamed.

Hands grabbed her from behind, pulling her away. Then she was in the air as she was thrown from the man she'd attacked. She landed hard, rolling in the dirt, and it forced the air out of her lungs. Pain exploded through her body from the rough landing on her side and she gasped, fighting for breath.

Brandi tried to recover, the battle to breathe taking up all her energy. The man on the ground cursed loudly. When he tore his hands away from where he clutched his face, she saw deep scratches on his eyelids and around his eyes. She'd nailed him but not as badly as she'd hoped. She'd wanted to permanently blind the son of a bitch.

Bleeding and panting heavily, he curled back his lip and growled at her. Literally growled like a dog. The sound was so odd it shocked her.

She was still gaping when a hand fisted in the hair at the base of her neck. She could only make a whimpering sound as the stranger painfully hauled Brandi to her feet, making her feel as if her hair had just been ripped out at the root.

She started fighting the excruciating hold he had on her hair, but she stopped short when she saw the other two men who'd come out of the woods.

As she stared, a third man pulled up in her car. The sense of dread nearly overwhelmed her when he got out of it, because she knew no cops were going to come looking for her now. There was no proof she was gone from the gas station. It would take days for them to find her car abandoned in the woods.

She looked around at the dirt road and the trees surrounding her, making her feel alone and isolated.

The man she'd attempted to blind got to his feet and stormed at her with pure rage etched on his marred face. Brandi tried to run instinctively, but the one holding her wrenched her head back so hard her neck throbbed. Trapped, she cowered from the attack, but one of the new arrivals, a man in his forties, jumped in the way.

"No, Chuck. You can't kill her." The man snarled the words harshly. "You wanna tear her up, then you do it by winning the right."

Chuck pointed wildly to his face, his voice more a growl than anything. "Look at what the cunt did to me!"

"I see." The older man nodded, looking vaguely impressed. "Stop crying. It will heal by tonight. She's got fight to her. That's a good thing. We want one like her. It'll make the hunt more challenging. Working for it makes the victory taste better."

Hunt? Terror filled Brandi. What in the hell was the older man talking about? She knew the answer wasn't anything she really wanted to know.

She studied the five men in the small clearing. Four of them watched her in return, something dark and sinister swirling in their gazes. The older man slowly turned and Brandi met a pair of icy green eyes. He had scars on his face. He was tall, over six feet, and wore sweatpants. She realized they were all wearing mismatched sweats and T-shirts, which was as odd as everything else that had happened.

"She gets a fifteen-minute head start," the older man decreed as he stared into Brandi's eyes, appraising her as if she were a piece of meat rather than a human being. "Then the hunt begins. The first one to catch her owns the kill. We're here to leave those damn Nightwinds a message. Be vicious. Rip her to shreds. Don't just eat her, spread the parts around, but leave her head alone. They need to know it was a woman. I want them to look at her face. When you're done, remember to head south and cross the river carefully so you don't leave a trail to follow home. I'll clean up this area and meet you where we discussed. Don't mess around longer than you need to. Be out of the woods well before dark. From our intel, no pack should be this way until nightfall. They'll find her when they come for the pack run."

Brandi almost collapsed to her knees but the man holding her hair made it impossible. Shock tore through her. They were going to hunt her? Like an animal? Who the hell were these crazy bastards? They were sick, twisted, and insane. Eat her? Rip her to shreds? She wanted to start screaming, but bile rose in her throat instead

"Why fifteen minutes?" a young, gangling man in his late teens asked while staring at Brandi's breasts.

"She's human. She'll be slow. We don't want this to be too easy. This is also a learning exercise. Some of you have forgotten your hunting instincts, being forced to live in the city. You've grown soft and our pack has taken too many hits to afford your laziness. A human to stalk will motivate you to remember what the hell you are, and teach you to use your natural abilities to track her. This territory will belong to us once we take out this damn pack."

The younger guy looked grim, as if Brandi had turned from a fun sport into homework. "Fine." He reached up and tugged off his shirt.

Brandi fought against the urge to throw up as men started to remove their shoes and clothing while their sadistic teacher folded his arms over his chest, looking annoyed and impatient.

The one holding Brandi's hair released her and stepped back as he also started to undress. She knew she should run but was abruptly frozen with terror.

The older man eyed her, an evil grin tugging at his lips. "Don't move until I tell you. Then you better run like the wind, little doe." His smile broadened. "Not that you have a chance to escape, but maybe if you run fast and far enough, they'll kill you in a fit of rage rather than rape you. The faster you run, the more carnal they'll be, and the more you'll look like a helpless animal instead of a hot piece of ass to play with."

She stared in horror at the four totally naked men, now ready to hunt her. This had to be a nightmare. She silently prayed someone would wake her ass up. Shit like this didn't happen, but it was all startlingly real.

She stared in numb shock as the naked men dropped to their hands and knees. What were they going to do now? It was like a satanic ritual as they bowed their heads and arched their backs, as if they were praying to the devil they were all cruel and insane enough to worship.

This couldn't be happening — she was seeing things.

Brandi backed up and would have fallen on her ass if the older man hadn't grabbed her, forcing her to stop moving. His fingers tangled in her hair as his other hand wrenched her arm behind her back, holding her immobile. He chuckled in her ear as she blinked rapidly.

They must have given her drugs. What she was seeing couldn't really be happening. Her mind silently screamed that it wasn't possible.

"Oh yes, it's real." The man laughed. "The hair. The bones cracking and shifting. The way their faces are changing and their bodies are reforming. You're seeing a miracle of nature. Watch as they totally transform into wolves." He yanked hard on her hair. "Werewolves are real." His voice lowered to an amused rumble. "Surprise."

Brandi stumbled and backed into a tree when he released her. She gawked at the four sets of eyes locked on her, cunning and hungry, making her actually feel like prey. Two of the wolves bared vicious-looking teeth and growled at her. She stared at them, open-mouthed. A strangled whimper slipped past her lips, echoing over the throb of fear that had her entire body tight with horror-induced adrenaline.

"Run, little doe," the older man yelled at her. "Run for your life!"

She gawked at him for a few seconds. That's how long it took her to realize he'd spoken to her.

She was the doe. Something to chase, attack and kill, without remorse.

In that moment, she fully comprehended the full scope of her horrific situation and it forced feeling into her numb, shaking body. She turned and ran as though the hounds of hell were on her ass — because they were.

****

Brandi didn't stop running.

She barely paused to breathe while she made her way blindly through the forest. She'd been pushing herself past the limits of her endurance for what felt like hours now.

No amount of wishing for a fresh start to the day was going to change what happened, and she refused to roll over and quit. She was going to collapse instead. Her body was exhausted. Her lungs burned. Her side was seized with knife-stabbing pain. She could hear something coming behind her, getting closer, even over her ragged breathing and pounding heartbeat. The sound of paws against the mossy ground was undeniable. The panting of a terrifying wolf made all the fine hairs on her arms stand on end.

Something hit her in the back. She went flying forward. Even before she landed on her stomach, Brandi knew she was about to die.

She hit the grass hard, her hands barely saving her face from taking most of the impact. A growl sounded from behind as she lay on the forest floor, gasping and struggling for air.

She turned her head. One of the large wolves was about five feet away, panting from the chase. She tried to crawl, forcing her body to keep moving. Leaves, dirt, and grass slipped through her fingers as she clawed violently at the earth. She saw the wolf move forward, stalking her with its teeth bared. He growled. His front legs lowered and tensed. He was going to attack. She took a deep breath, screamed, and rolled as the wolf leaped at her.

He barely missed landing on her body. She'd moved just in time. With both hands she flung her fistfuls of earth, desperate for a reprieve from the evitable. She was lucky. The dirt hit him in the face. He made a whining sound and jerked away as he brought up a paw and rubbed at his eyes.

Not knowing how she found the strength, Brandi dragged herself up and ran again. She was going to die in the woods. She knew the wolf would recover. She didn't know how much longer she was going to survive. Not long, judging by the way her body was slowing. She wasn't in the best of shape. She had a treadmill but her limit was two miles. She had never run this fast or this hard in her life.

She heard a sound and turned to look back. A wolf was coming up behind her quickly. Overtaking her was easy — but then he sped up and crossed in front of her, blocking Brandi's escape.

She turned and tripped on a thigh-high furry body, dropping like dead weight.

Brandi was too exhausted to lessen the fall and landed painfully. Two wolves surrounded her, growling and showing their teeth. She rolled on her back, panting, and the struggle to breathe made everything seemed hazed. Even with so little oxygen, she still managed a piercing scream of horror.

One of the two brown wolves hunched his front legs and then launched at her. She tensed and tried to roll away but she could barely move. She stared in horror at the large wolf coming at her.

This was it. They were going to tear her apart with their sharp teeth.

Before he could attack, a black wolf seemed to appear out of nowhere, hitting the other wolf coming down on her and knocking him to the ground.

She blinked, still fighting for clarity as the two wolves rolled over each other, a swirl of brown and black fur as vicious snarling and growling filled the air.

She watched in shock, realizing the wolves were fighting, and it was a brutal battle, especially when the other brown wolf jumped into the fray. The two brown wolves were clearly trying to gang up on the black one, but she wasn't so sure they were winning. That black wolf was noticeably bigger, and he was definitely faster. She saw blood and fur fly before she started gathering her bearings.

Brandi rolled, crawling away from the gory fight, and managed to get to her feet. She stumbled. The world swayed wildly and she couldn't get a clear look at anything, but she started running again. She didn't know why they were attacking each other and she didn't care.

She heard snarls and whines coming from behind, and against her better judgment, turned back to look, wanting to see how much time she had. Unexpectedly, she slammed into a low branch and found herself flat on her back once more.

The pain in her head was excruciating, forcing Brandi to fight the blackness that threatened. She touched her forehead, feeling something wet and warm. She lifted her arm, seeing blood dripping off her fingers, and then tried to get up but a wave of dizziness hit. She collapsed and lay there as the world started to fade to gray.

Trying to fight against passing out, she turned on her side, looking back once more. The three wolves were still fighting, jaws snapping as they rolled on the ground, leaving splatters of blood in their wake. The two smaller brown wolves were still ganging up on the bigger black one, who really was an impressive wolf, broader and more powerful than all the others she'd seen.

With a furious growl, she saw him grab the neck of one of the brown wolves. A loud whine rent the air when the black wolf shook his head savagely, his teeth buried deep. Blood flew everywhere. Then the black wolf tossed the now limp wolf aside and turned on the remaining brown wolf, who was biting at his hind leg.

Her eyes went to the prone wolf on the ground. She could see that his throat had been ripped open. Blood pooled around the unmoving body. The black wolf had killed it. He'd torn out its throat and threw it away from the fight.

In seconds, the black wolf batted out a paw, tearing open one side of the other brown wolf's face.

The injured wolf howled in agony, but the cry was cut off as the black wolf bit into its throat. There was a sickening crunching sound, more blood flew, spraying the black wolf and the earth, and then the brown wolf went still.

The black wolf released its dead prey and turned.

He stared at her as he took slow steps toward Brandi, and she couldn't look away. His fur was midnight black. He had hypnotizing brown eyes, the color of warm chocolate, a complete contrast to his otherwise deadly aura. He took another step and Brandi moaned in fear. She touched the bleeding spot on the left side of her forehead, knowing he was about to tear her throat out next.

He stopped and sniffed the air. Then lifted his head and let out a howl. It was a long one, loud and eerie. It left a warning in the air that was hard to ignore.

Brandi was surprised when another brown wolf ran into view a few seconds later, obviously realizing his mistake as he came to a skidding halt. Too late—the black wolf attacked as the brown one backed up, trying to turn and run.

Brandi swore she saw panic and fear in the pale green eyes of the new arrival. It wasn't without merit. He was dead before he had a chance to realize what was about to happen. The black wolf had gone right for his neck, grabbing him, and tearing out his throat in one violent clamp of sharp teeth and a strong shake of the head. The black wolf seemed to spit out the blood as it threw the dead wolf's body aside.

Tears filled Brandi's eyes, and she wasn't even sure what was causing her to fall over the edge. There were so many reasons, it was impossible to pinpoint. The black wolf slowly turned and took a step toward her. She tried to get up but all she got for her trouble was a wave of dizziness. The pain in her head was so sharp she almost blacked out again. She stopped moving and just stared into the black wolf's warm eyes.

He moved in closer, pausing about four feet from her and tilting his head curiously.

Then he did something surprising—he wagged his tail.

She felt a wave of confusion wash over her as the deadly wolf shut his mouth, his tail now wagging furiously. He made a soft whining sound and then slowly inched closer to her. He lowered his head and kept wagging his tail like an offer of friendship.

She closed her eyes, fighting hard for clarity. She took a few breaths and then forced her eyes open. The black wolf was almost touching her. She could have reached up and stroked his face. He was a big damn dog.

Wolf, she corrected. He had to be two hundred pounds at least, certainly bigger than any dog she'd ever seen, with his thick body and muscular chest and legs. He blinked…and then his face started to change.

The long snout began to shorten. The hair on his face receded. His body shifted from being on all fours to sitting down so he sat on his back legs. His paws turned into deeply tanned hands. She couldn't look away as the wolf changed into a naked, muscular, tan man with the same midnight-black hair. Even kneeling, he was noticeably tall and powerfully built.

Intimidating on a primal level.

Incredible, beautiful brown eyes the shade of chocolate stared at her from beneath a pair of long, thick eyelashes.

He stretched out his hand toward her.

A big, powerful human hand.

He touched her, and she would have screamed if she weren't frozen with shock. His caress was surprisingly warm and soothing as he stroked her forehead.

"It's going to be all right." His voice was deep and husky, like expensive whiskey. "You're safe."

Enthralled, she was too dazed to look away. He had strong cheekbones and a granite-hard jaw that had gone a few days without shaving. She saw dark whiskers on his chin. He had a cut on his full bottom lip and he wiped away the blood impatiently as though it was nothing.

She noticed a tattoo on his shoulder, but she couldn't see exactly what it was because of how his body was turned. A sheen of sweat covered his skin. His arms were as thick and defined as the rest of him. His stomach was rock hard and she could see the deep lines of his abdominal muscles. This wolf was massive as a human. Beefy and muscular and just wide all over.

Her gaze dipped lower and she was shocked to find him totally naked and undeniably aroused. This guy really *was* large and wide all over.

Her gaze flew up to meet his once more.

"I've got you. I'm going to pick you up. My place isn't too far from here. You're safe now. I killed them."

She opened her mouth but nothing came out. She was obviously in extreme shock if she was noticing this guy's muscles and hard-on. She wanted to say something. Maybe scream? She wasn't sure which. All she managed to do was mutely study him. He slipped one of his hands under her back and hooked his other arm behind her knees. He lifted her into his arms as he stood.

She felt a wave of dizziness again. The man was staring into her eyes, confusing her with the feeling of comfort that look caused. She felt blackness coming and this time she didn't fight it. She was living in a nightmare and she wanted an escape. Sleep seemed the only option, and she gave in to it.

Chapter Two

For one split second, Jason thought she'd died.

His chest tightened with fear as he cocked his head, listening for a heartbeat. He breathed a sigh of relief when he heard it, finding it steady, if not a little fast despite the fact that she was completely unconscious.

He wasn't sure if she'd passed out from shock or injury, and he wasn't going to wait around to figure it out. Walking fast, he carried her back toward his cabin on the edge of the pack's territory. He lived on the outskirts of pack land by design, so he could patrol and protect the northern border from wolves stupid enough to trespass, like the ones he'd just eliminated.

Still feeling furious and feral, Jason's lip curled back and he growled low in his throat when he thought of those wolves attacking this small, curvy woman. Her light brown hair was long and wildly curly. Even dirty and tangled with leaves, it felt soft as it tickled his bare thigh. Her face appeared almost angelic, her lips full, pink, and tempting. He would've thought they'd been chasing her for sex, considering how aggressive male wolves could be when they were after a sweet-smelling female.

The Weres' methods of seduction weren't exactly socially acceptable in human society.

Forcing a human female was forbidden in their culture, but chasing after one for the chance to convince a prospective mate of their strength and cunning happened more than it should. It would've been easy to understand a few young, untrained wolves pursuing a pretty female into another pack's territory, but those wolves hadn't been after her for her curves, and this wasn't a bitch in heat. This female was one hundred percent human—and they'd been hunting to kill.

Jason growled again, this time louder and more territorial as he looked down at the cut on her forehead that still bled. He wished he could go back and kill those bastards again just for the fun of it.

When he reached his cabin, he kicked at the door that had been left partially open when he ran out after hearing the woman's screams.

He walked to the fireplace that still had a strong blaze going. He'd been roasting some rabbit he'd caught this morning for lunch, and now it was too burnt to be edible, but that was the least of his worries. At least he hadn't burned the place down.

He laid the human gently on the large couch in front of the fire and covered her. Hoping she'd rest more comfortably, he took off her shoes and socks, but left the rest of her clothes on because he knew humans were strangely shy about their skin.

She didn't stir, which worried him. He sniffed her in concern once he'd put her shoes aside, looking for the stench of death that could cling to the gravely injured, but he didn't smell a life-threatening injury. She actually smelled nice, in a human sort of way. Even under the layers of dirt and blood, she had a sweet, wholly feminine scent that set off every protective instinct Jason had.

Those rogue wolves died far too quickly. Not for the first time, he wished he'd thought to make them suffer first.

He brushed some of the curls away from her face gently, wondering why they'd been after her. Everything about her scent compelled him. It was soft, inviting enough to make his skin tingle. She was startling beautiful for a human, more so than any of the others he'd come across. Not that he sought them out that often. He knew them well enough, hell, he was part human, but Jason's past taught him that his kind didn't blend well with humans.

He dropped his gaze to her chest, using the excuse of inspecting her breathing to eye her breasts that were lush and tempting — too tempting.

He stood, feeling more than a little uncomfortable checking out an unconscious woman who was obviously having a very bad day. He understood enough about the human culture to know she wouldn't appreciate having a big, dirty, slightly bloody and extremely naked Were hovering over her if she woke. Especially one who'd sported a rock-hard dick since the moment he'd laid eyes on her.

Needing something to do with his hands that were itching to wake her up in a way she probably wouldn't appreciate, Jason pulled on a pair of jeans. It wasn't an easy task with the raging hard-on he was dealing with. He used a washcloth to clean his lip that still bled. Then he threw out the burnt rabbit. She'd probably give him some shit about killing Thumper. For all he knew, she could be a vegetarian.

Jason shuddered. One of many reasons why humans confused him.

Even as he went through the mental list of reasons why a human female was completely off-limits, he found himself hovering back over her. This time he covered her with a blanket as he studied her round, angelic face and worriedly touched the cut on her forehead.

The sight of it bothered him so much, he found himself leaning down to lick the wound to help it heal faster. He was fairly certain it'd work on a human just as easily as it would on another Were. Then he stroked her hair softly as he sniffed at the curve of her neck and listened more intently to the steady beat of her heart.

The protective instincts washed over him stronger than ever.

Jason shot to his feet. The foreign sensations surging through his bloodstream made him feel angry and irrational that this woman had almost died in the forest. In Nightwind territory. *My territory.*

He didn't know why those wolves were hunting her, but he was going to make damn sure it didn't happen again.

He walked into the kitchen and grabbed his cell phone off the counter. He called one of the pack alphas, his leg twitching as he waited for it to ring. It went to voice mail. He'd have to leave a message and hope it was returned sooner rather than later.

Jason ran a hand through his hair and craned his neck to stare at the sleeping human on his couch. "Des, we've got a major problem."

After he was done, Jason decided to go upstairs and take a very cold shower. Not only to wash away the dirt and blood from the fight, but hopefully find his common sense while he was at it.

****

Brandi's head hurt. Lying on something soft, she was covered up and warm. Curious, she opened her eyes and found herself staring at a crackling fireplace with red and gold flames dancing over the logs behind the grate. She inhaled the scent of burning wood and something else, the rustic aroma of cooked meat.

She looked around without moving, finding the raw masculinity of the small area completely foreign. She'd never been in this room before.

"There were three of them, Des." It was a whiskey-rough voice speaking softly from somewhere. "I don't know what the hell they were doing in our territory but they weren't just messing around with this woman. They were out for her blood, and I didn't recognize any of those wolves. That's what I can't figure out. Why the hell were they going after a human woman? It makes zero fucking sense."

She knew that voice. Memories of a big, powerful black wolf turning into a sexy man in his mid-thirties with warm brown eyes flickered in the back of her mind, amidst flashes of a nightmare come to life.

"She took a big bump to the head and she's scratched up. I thought about taking her to the hospital, but she had no identification on her. I don't know what her story is. I'd like to keep her here until we know more. I can protect her. If I took her to a hospital, it could lead more of them to her if they're still hunting her, and we know they probably are."

Silence followed, making it obvious he was listening on the phone. Somehow she knew he was the only other person in the house and was simply waiting for whoever he was talking to on the other end to say their piece.

Then she heard him huff in frustration. "She's very attractive, but they came at her in fur, Desmon. This wasn't about raping her. I barely got to her in time. Two of them were about to tear her apart. I caught one of them in mid-strike. It was a killing attack. Send a few of our guys out to clean up the area and scout it out to make sure there aren't more. I'm going to find out who she is and see what the hell's going on."

Silence once more, then a deep sigh. "I'll feed her when she wakes, and try to get some answers. Tonight, I'll slip something into her drink so she sleeps through the night. We'll meet up at the scheduled run. I better get off here now. She could wake up at any time."

Brandi heard a click after a quick goodbye, and then a chair creaked. She looked toward a door, which probably led to a kitchen. A good minute passed. Then she saw the man from the woods walk into the living room. He was drinking something from a mug, probably coffee.

He'd showered. His short black hair was wet and pushed away from his face. He had a small cut on his bottom lip, but otherwise he looked almost too perfect standing there shirtless in only a pair of snug, faded blue jeans that hung low on his hips. His feet were bare and she stared at the sheer size of them until he suddenly stopped walking. She instinctively looked up and his brown gaze locked with hers.

"Hey," he said softly as he loomed over her, big, powerful and wholly intimidating. "You're safe here. I need you to know that. You're protected."

She swallowed. She didn't try to speak. She just stared at him as terror flooded her system and memories of the hunt bombarded her mind.

He inhaled, his nose flaring a little before he frowned. "You're frightened and it's understandable. I know you were attacked by wolves, but they won't come after you here. They'd never come close to my home. I promise you that you're safe now." He crouched down next to the couch and offered her his coffee mug. "Do you want a drink? It's hot coffee. Maybe it'll help you wake up."

She struggled to sit up despite her apprehension. This stranger was huge and she'd seen him turn from a black wolf into a man. Had she been drugged when the men grabbed her from the gas station? She couldn't possibly have seen this man as a wolf.

Her head throbbed and it made her thinking fuzzy. Jason silently watched her, still offering his coffee, and she felt like she needed it. She wasn't super excited about sharing a drink with this stranger, but she was desperate to wake up a little. Her hands shook as she reached for the coffee.

He turned the mug and offered her the handle. "Careful. It's hot. I don't want you to get burned."

NIGHTWIND PACK: CLAIMED 37

His large palms closed over hers as she brought the coffee to her lips. She stared at him as she blew a little and then took a sip of the coffee. It *was* hot, but it didn't burn her. She was still shaking and she was grateful for the big warm hands holding her steady as she took another sip. She had seen him drink from it so she was sure the coffee wasn't drugged, but she'd heard him admit that he was planning on drugging her later. As kind as he was being now, she couldn't allow herself to forget that. She pushed the cup away.

He took it and set it on the coffee table, before he turned back to her

"I'm Jason. What's your name?"

She hesitated, studying him uncertainly before she shrugged. "Brandi Compro."

"What were you doing in the woods, Brandi?"

She hesitated again, and then decided to tell him the truth. He'd rescued her. Regardless of the fogged memories she had about Jason as a wolf, one way or another he'd obviously saved her, since she was safe on his couch rather than scattered in pieces across the forest floor.

"I was grabbed from a gas station. Two men in a white cargo van kidnapped me."

Jason's mouth pressed together in a tight line. "Have you ever seen those men before? Do you know them?"

"Never. I'm not from this area. I was driving to see my best friend, Jenny. Her place's five hours from where I live. I pulled off the highway in Dryer for gas. They grabbed me, threw me in the back of the van, and I was locked in like an animal. There was a cage wall between the front and back of the van. The doors wouldn't open."

"What happened next?"

She stared into his soft brown eyes and remembered the black wolf once more. "I think they drugged me."

"Did they make you swallow pills or put a rag over your face?" His voice was lower, more of a growl. "Did they inject you with something?"

She felt her cheeks heat and lowered her head as she admitted, "No. It's just... I saw things that weren't real. That *couldn't* be real."

He breathed a small sigh of relief but didn't say a word, just waited silently as she tried to find a way to tell him the twisted story.

"They drove me into a clearing in the woods and opened the van door. I tackled one of them and clawed his eyes with my fingernails."

Shock crossed his features before he let his gaze drift over her body in a long, lingering look before he lifted his head and narrowed his eyes suspiciously. "You attacked one of them?"

"I know I'm not very strong looking, but I have an older brother. He taught me how to fight. He said I needed to be strong to protect myself. I figured they were going to rape and kill me, so I backed up in the van and when one of them opened the doors, I shoved off from the side and barreled into him. I had the advantage. I was higher and he wouldn't have expected me to come out like that. When I landed on him, I went for his eyes. The other man pulled me off the one I hurt. Then I realized there were five of them and—"

He frowned. "Five? Not three? Are you sure?"

"Five. Trust me. I'll never forget it. There was an older man. He seemed to be in charge. He didn't come after me into the woods. He…" She chewed on her bottom lip, studying the man crouched on the floor within feet of her. Jason was close enough to touch and she found herself itching to do it. She folded her hands in her lap to fight the odd impulse as she winced over the memories. "He freaked me out the worst. He was like their fucked-up teacher or something."

"What made you think that?"

"Because of what he said. I was supposed to be a learning exercise. He said they had gotten too soft or some such bullshit. I was in shock so don't quote me." She held up her hands, giving him a look because she knew this all sounded insane. She had a feeling she'd be in a white jacket already if she told the police what she was telling Jason.

"He told them to hunt me like an animal. He called me a doe. Whoever reached me first got the kill. He wanted them to—" She shuddered, lowering her head once more as her voice caught. "They were supposed to tear me up and scatter my body parts. He ordered them to leave my head alone so it was obvious I was a woman when the Nightwinds found my body tonight, whatever that means. Then they were supposed to be out of the woods by dark because that's when my body would be found. This all sounds crazy, I know, but—"

Brandi looked up and saw real anger tightening Jason's face. He looked furious enough to frighten her. She tensed and pressed her back tightly to the couch, but she couldn't go anywhere else since Jason was still crouched in front of her. He blinked and then his harsh features relaxed.

"Did you catch any names?"

"Just one. Chuck. He's the one I scratched up when I jumped out of the van."

"What did the older man look like?"

"Ice-cold green eyes. They were freaky looking." She stared into Jason's warm brown eyes to fight the shudder the memory caused, not that she should feel any safer around him, but she did for some reason. "Cold and just evil. He had some scars on his face." She touched her cheek, still caught in the nightmare. "Here, here and here. He was about fifty-something, in good shape, maybe six feet tall. Oh, and he had marks on his left arm. They were about two inches apart and went from under his T-shirt sleeve down to his elbow. I saw three of them." She touched her arm to show him. "Scars."

"I don't know him. Damn. That's bad. If I knew him, we could take care of him for good, and I could promise you he wouldn't be attacking any more women. They used the term 'hunt' or did you come up with that one?"

"That was his term. He said they were going to hunt me. He gave me a fifteen-minute head start and laughed." The shock was wearing off and she was getting pissed off. "*He laughed.* He was amused over them hunting me like a deer. He told them to tear me apart. I don't even know this jerkoff. They even stole my car and hid it in the woods so no one would know to look for me."

She took a deep breath, the anger making her forget just how crazy her story sounded. "I need your phone. I need to call the police. To call my friend Jenny. She'll be worried that I didn't show up."

He hesitated and looked away for the first time. "My phone is down. We had a storm a few days ago. I don't carry a cell phone. I'm sorry."

He was lying, and Brandi glared long enough for him to look back to her. The guilt showed on his handsome face as he let his gaze run over her once more, as if trying to hide from her disappointment. "Do you want a shower?"

She looked down at herself. Her shirt was torn in a few places and dirty. Her khaki shorts had tears and were beyond filthy. She saw red stains mixed in with the grass and dirt, and touched them, feeling the color leave her face. It was dried blood smeared over all her clothing and she fingered her shorts in horror.

"What else happened? You said you thought they gave you drugs."

She stared at him, but didn't say a word.

"Brandi? What made you think they gave you drugs?"

She moved fast, her bare foot making contact with his naked chest. She had no idea what happened to her shoes and she wasn't going to worry about it when she kicked him hard enough to send him crashing into the coffee table.

Brandi jumped off the couch as she heard glass break and Jason's loud cursing. She sprinted for the front door, pulling it open wildly before dashing outside. Finding nothing but forest, she ran toward the black SUV parked in front of the cabin.

She reached it and jerked on the door, only to find it locked.

"Where are you going to go, Brandi?"

She gasped and spun to see Jason directly behind her. She backed up and leaned against the truck. "Stay away. You're lying to me. You have a working phone or a cell phone or something. I just heard you talking on it. You're planning on drugging me later!"

"Shit." Jason sighed. "You heard that?"

She just grunted in response, eyeing him fearfully. She couldn't get over how wide-shouldered and muscular he was, which was unfortunate when she considered having to fight him to get free. Jason had one of the best bodies she'd ever seen. The guy had to work out often to get that kind of body mass and definition, that was more than obvious, since he wasn't wearing a shirt. Every muscle was ridged down his stomach to the waist of his faded jeans.

She could make out his tattoo this time, the silhouette of a wolf howling at the moon in black ink on his arm, with the word *Nightwind* written under it. It was simple, making it look more like a brand.

Not good.

"I told you that you're safe here." Jason reached out to her, but she flinched and he dropped his arm. "I was going to give you something to help you sleep so I could leave you alone. The woods aren't safe to roam in, and I was afraid you'd try to leave after I went out tonight to hunt for the other men who brought you to my territory."

She flinched again. *Hunt. Just like those other men. He hunts. Did I really see him change from a wolf into a man? Oh god!* Her mind reeled as she tried to flatten herself against the SUV in a vain attempt to get out of this situation.

Jason inhaled deeply and took a few steps back. He lifted his hands, palms out, and then backed up a little more. "Easy, Brandi. You're terrified and there's no reason to be. I'm not going to hurt you."

"I saw." She pointed at him accusingly.

Jason blinked, paling a little despite his tan skin. "What did you see?"

She inched along the SUV to the back. "They stripped out of their clothes in front of me and went down on their hands and knees." She cleared her throat, her voice a hushed whisper. "I saw. They changed in front of me…and then I saw *you*. You were the black wolf."

Jason moved with her, inching sideways, but didn't come closer to her as they stared at each other. "That's why you think you were drugged." It wasn't a question. "You know you've got a nasty bump on your forehead."

She made a soft sound in her throat. "That's what I thought until I saw the blood on my clothes. I thought they'd drugged me or I hit my head too hard, but the blood doesn't lie. You killed those wolves and you changed into a man. Then you lifted me. You were covered in their blood." She glanced down at her clothes and then her head jerked up. "It really happened. The proof's staining my clothes."

"Easy," Jason said softly. "Don't panic. I see it in your eyes. You're not in danger, Brandi. I won't hurt you."

Brandi turned and ran.

She heard Jason curse behind her as she took off down the dirt road. There had to be a main road at the bottom.

She was running downhill and she didn't hear anything behind her. Her bare feet pounded along the soft dirt. Her body ached from her previous run, but she needed to get to a main road. She could flag someone down and call the police. She needed to get away from the man who swore she was safe because she knew she wasn't.

Two arms locked around her waist and she was forced back into a hard wall of bare skin and rough jeans. Her feet left the ground. She screamed and tried to throw her head back to hit him in the face, but Jason tilted his chin out of the way and her head slammed into his chest instead.

"Damn it," he rasped. "Don't fight me! You're so little. I don't want to accidentally hurt you."

She screamed out again and clawed at the arms banded around her waist like warm iron. Jason cursed loudly as she raked her nails across his skin. She knew she scored blood. He shifted her weight in his arms and put her on her feet. Brandi tried to kick him as he yanked her off her feet again and into his arms. He turned and started walking back to the cabin.

"Let me go!" she shouted, more than a little nervous that he'd drop her because she wasn't exactly a pixie.

"Calm down." He crooned. "It's not safe for you to be running around. You're going to have to deal with me until

I'm sure you're safe. You said it yourself. You saw their faces. The older man you described will hunt you until he's certain you're dead. Believe it or not, I'm the best friend you've got in these woods."

She stopped struggling. It was useless. Kicking didn't seem to faze him and he was incredibly strong. He wasn't hurting her or crushing her to keep her still. She could feel his muscles since she was locked in his arms. Never in her life had she felt more tiny and weak as he carried her back to the cabin, and it was infuriating.

The front door was wide open. He walked inside, turned, and used his foot to kick the door shut. Then he headed for the stairs.

"You need a shower. I'm going to take you to the guest bathroom. It's the only one with a window too small to crawl out of. It's pretty bare but I do have towels and soap and stuff you can use to get cleaned up. I'll get you some clothes, and then we'll talk. Don't try to escape. I really don't want to accidentally hurt you."

He walked to the first door on the right, down the hall from four other closed doors. He gently stood Brandi on her feet, but refused to let her go completely. One massive hand gripped her upper arm as he reached over and flipped on a light in the bathroom. It only had a toilet, sink, and open shower stall. He gently pushed her into the shower and released her. He gripped the frame of the stall as Brandi backed away from him.

His brown gaze locked with hers. "Take a shower. There's shampoo, conditioner, and even a few new toothbrushes in the drawer. I'll leave you some clothes in the hallway. There's a lock on the door. Use it if you want, but it's not necessary. I've never forced a woman in my life and I am not about to start now. Shower, calm down, and then we'll talk. I'll fix you something to eat. I can hear your stomach rumbling." He stepped back and shut the shower stall. "I'm out here, so don't try to escape again."

Brandi lunged and flipped the lock once he'd left the bathroom. She tested the door, making sure it really was secured. She heard a soft male chuckle from the other side of the door.

Brandi backed up and sat down on the toilet lid, shaking from head to toe.

Chapter Three

Now clean, with her skin rosy from being scrubbed nearly raw to get the dirt and blood off, Brandi had to admit she felt better as she studied herself in the mirror. The towel was wrapped tightly around her body. Her long wet hair was already bouncing back to its usual curly, unruly state. Her light blue eyes were rimmed with dark circles. She had a bump on her forehead with a thin, healing cut running through the center of it, but it still had to be an improvement over how she'd looked before.

She touched the wound, surprised that it was tinged green rather than black and blue. Usually it took a week for bad bruises to fade. Maybe she hadn't hit her head as hard as she'd thought.

Brandi shrugged and decided to brush her teeth with the new toothbrush and toothpaste she found in the drawer. She did feel a hundred times better and more like herself, but she still found herself eyeing the door with dread after she finished brushing her teeth. She'd have to unlock it, and see if he'd left her clothes. Was it a trick? Would he be waiting to grab her?

Jason hadn't attacked her yet. And she'd been unconscious. If he were a pervert, wouldn't he have taken advantage of her then? He hadn't picked the lock and trapped her naked in the shower. A monster would have done that.

She sighed and walked to the door and pressed her ear against. When she heard only silence, she bit her lip and reached for the knob. She unlocked it, tensed, and when nothing happened, she eased the door open.

The hallway stood empty. She looked down and saw neatly folded clothing on the floor. She grabbed the clothes and slammed the bathroom door shut and locked it. Her heart pounded as she put the clothes on the counter.

The T-shirt he gave her smelled like fabric softener, and it was easily two times too big for her, but it was warm and soft. She tugged it down her body, letting it fall past her knees. She frowned as she picked up the second and last piece of clothing. It wasn't pants. It was a pair of black cotton boxer briefs. Men's. She uttered a soft curse and put them on.

They were a little big but they fit. She lifted the shirt and stared in the mirror. She'd never worn men's underwear before. They were soft and comfortable. She sighed and dropped the shirt. At least she was covered and the clothes were clean.

A tap on the door made her jump.

"Hey, you hungry yet or are you going to hide out in there all day? Did everything fit? I would have given you pants but my jeans would fall off you and my sweats will probably tell the same story."

She stared at the door and sighed. "I don't know if I want to come out or not. You're a liar at best and a crazy wolf-man at worst. With my luck, you're both."

He chuckled. "Yeah. I lied to you. I have a phone. I just can't let you use it, but I'll tell you what. You come out and eat something with me and I won't lie to you anymore."

She crossed her arms over her chest. "You were the black wolf, weren't you?"

Seconds ticked by. "Yeah. That's me, Brandi. I'm a wolf. I'm not crazy though. Even if it sounds like it, I promise I'm not."

"Are you actually admitting you were a real wolf or are you humoring me?" She couldn't hide her shock.

"What did you see?"

"I saw you go from being a black wolf to becoming a naked man."

"I admitted I'm the wolf. What more do you want?"

She walked to the door and leaned her forehead against it. "How is that possible? What are you?"

Brandi knew he was in the hallway, but she didn't realize how close he was until he spoke softly against the other side of the door. "Come out and I'll tell you everything. You're safe with me. I won't hurt you. I saved you, remember?"

She'd never forget that fight in the woods. He did save her life. He killed those other terrible creatures. He hadn't hurt her yet. In fact, he'd been oddly considerate.

She sighed and flipped the lock before opening the door slowly, still questioning her sanity for trusting him.

Jason had backed up to lean against the opposite wall

"Hi." He gave her a smile, showing off dimples beneath the scruff of whiskers that made him look dangerously handsome. "You still hungry?" His eyebrows rose as stared at her standing there in nothing but his shirt and hidden boxer briefs. "Sorry everything is so big. I don't have any women's clothing in my cabin. My shirt is almost like a dress on you. All that's missing is a belt and high heels."

"What are you?" she repeated, refusing to be swayed, no matter how compelling he was.

His smile faded. "A man."

She slowly shook her head in denial because they both knew that wasn't true.

He arched an eyebrow at her and gestured to his shirtless chest pointedly. "Take another look. I'm definitely a man."

Brandi couldn't help but stare like he suggested. He had an amazing body. Muscular, tan, perfect. She took a step into the hallway and looked up at his face. He was unbelievably handsome.

Sexy.

And he turned into a wolf…a deadly one.

Beneath the casual charm, she could still sense it. There was something wild and untamed about the powerful, enthralling man leaning against the wall.

Jason took a step toward her. "Touch me. I won't bite. I'm a man, Brandi. Flesh and blood like you. You can touch me. It's safe. I won't hurt you."

She lifted her hand and hoped he didn't notice it shook. She gently placed her hand on his stomach. It was warm and rock hard and definitely flesh. She traced her fingers lower and his stomach muscles clenched. She saw a fine sheen of goose bumps spread over the smooth skin. That seemed human, but...

"You still turn into a wolf."

"I do." His voice was low and raspy. "I was born that way. I'm a man and I'm more. I've never hurt a woman in my life. My father was like you. Just human. My mother was like me. She was more. He left when she was pregnant with me. I didn't know him, but I *am* half human, so we have that in common. I'm not totally different from you."

Brandi stared up at him. He was sharing personal things with her. She wondered why but she was grateful. It made him more normal to her. She let her hand drop and took a step back.

"There is a small population of us in the United States. I'm not the only one of my kind. Your people like to call us Werewolves, but there are a lot of fucked-up misconceptions about us. We're nothing like you see in the movies. Those ideas are mostly fantasy. The reality is we have families like you do. Jobs like you do. Friends like you do. Most of the time we're just trying to protect what's ours...like you do."

"Those other men wanted to kill me," she said uneasily. "Why? And why don't *you* want to kill me? What makes you different? Don't wolves hunt humans?"

"Those other wolves were assholes. I don't know why they wanted to hurt you. That is disturbingly fucked up and I can promise you that most of us don't go around kidnapping and killing innocent humans. If you'll eat, I'll try to explain to you why I think you were attacked."

She nodded in agreement, knowing she was probably horribly naïve for believing him, but she couldn't seem to help herself.

Jason turned, studied her carefully, and then walked for the stairs. He paused at the top. "Why don't you go first? I'd hate for you to kick me again and send me flying down the steps."

She flushed a little. "Sorry about the coffee table."

He grinned. "It's all right. Only the mug broke. The table survived. You're feisty. I like that. Besides, who am I to be mad at you for trying to defend yourself? It's a good trait to have. I do, however, wish you'd go first."

She moved around him and went down the stairs. He stayed behind her and motioned toward the kitchen. She smelled food and her stomach growled.

Jason touched the small of her back lightly. "Let's eat. I had some beef and vegetable soup left over, so I heated that up. I didn't want you to have to wait too long to get some food in you. It's homemade. Not from a can or anything."

He'd made turkey sandwiches to go with the soup. He must have been putting the meal together when she'd opened the hallway door to get her clothes. He pulled out a chair for her. She was surprised at his good manners and commented on it.

"My mother taught me to be a gentleman. We're in human form more often than not. My mother didn't raise an animal." He chuckled. "At least not most of the time." He took a chair across from her. "I poured milk. I hope that's all right?"

She nodded and dug into the soup. It was shockingly good. Brandi would've thought it was delicious even if she weren't starving. The turkey sandwiches were good too. She ate it all. Jason ate twice as much as she did. He'd polished off two bowls of soup and three sandwiches.

It was only when she found herself staring down at an empty plate and bowl that Brandi thought to be embarrassed with how fast she'd devoured the meal.

Her cheeks heated. "Thank you. That was really good."

"I'm an excellent cook. My mom always wanted a girl to pass down all the family recipes to, since both of her brothers died and she was the last of the line. Instead she got me." Jason shrugged casually. "So I got to be the son who learned everything, including Grandma Ellen's peach cobbler recipe and how to make a mean stew like my great-uncle Greg."

Brandi smiled. "I understand that to a degree. My dad wanted a boy. He got me instead. He signed me up for every sport he could. I'd had enough of it by the time I hit high school. He was ready to fight the school board to see if he could force me to be a football player, since they didn't accept girls."

A frown marred Jason's face. "I thought you said you had a brother."

She nodded. "I do. We have different fathers. My mom was married to Joe's dad. They divorced. She met my dad and got pregnant with me. My dad wanted to marry her but she was still in love with her ex-husband. They got back together. Joe and I were raised in the same house, but I spent weekends with my dad. He was active in my life and I'm his only child. He really wanted a boy. Joe always encouraged me to toughen up too. Even when I got older and lost interest in sports, he agreed with my dad. Not to be a jerk, he was just afraid boys would target me because…"

Jason arched an eyebrow when she stopped talking. "Because you're very attractive?"

"Thank you, but not really." She felt her cheeks heat once more because he sounded sincere in a way she hadn't heard from a man before. "I've never been skinny. Kids picked on me because I was short and round. Joe taught me how to defend myself since he couldn't always be there to protect me against the bullies."

"You're not overweight. You're lush. Feminine." Jason tilted his head, giving her another deep-dimpled smile. "I always thought that was one of the benefits of human women, their softness. I'm sure the men you know like that very much."

"I, um…" She paused, not sure how to respond to that, so she said, "Thank you, I think, but that's not totally true. It's much more socially acceptable to be thin. I've worked really hard at losing weight. I bought a treadmill, joined a gym, and got on one of those diet programs where you buy the food so I'd be slimmer for my wedding. I dropped twenty pounds and managed to fit into my dream dress."

He glanced at her hand. "No wedding rings? Did they steal them from you? You didn't mention needing to call a husband."

"I'm divorced. I married the wrong guy." She shrugged and lowered her gaze back to her plate. "We were married for just over a year before I realized what a domineering jerk he was. Carl was the one pushing me to lose the weight, so I should've known how shallow he was. The control trip was bad enough, but then I found out he was sleeping with other women. I left and never looked back. I still try to stay fit, but I'm just naturally *lush*, as you put it."

Jason nodded. "I see."

"What about you?" She glanced at his hand the same way he'd done to her. "No wedding ring?"

"Nope." He grinned. "Not yet. I haven't found the right one. I thought I did once but she couldn't handle my life."

"You mean your secret?"

"She was like me. That wasn't it. She didn't like my job. Being half human made it kind of tough growing up around full-blooded Weres. I had to fight a lot when the other males thought I was a pushover or weaker for my half-human genes. I got so good at fighting that no one could beat me. I was given my job because of it. I'm the law enforcement of my kind in this area. She didn't like that. She wanted a calmer life than being mated to an enforcer."

She took a shuddering breath as she remembered him saving her. "You fought and won against three other wolves."

"Yeah." He nodded. "Most of my kind couldn't win that kind of fight."

She couldn't help but look at his broad bare shoulders and powerful arms. "You're really in shape."

"Brandi." His voice caught with something seductive and compelling. "Don't look at me like that."

Her gaze flew up to his. Those earnest brown eyes had darkened as he studied her from across the table, making her feel like a completely different kind of prey. She moved in her seat as a warm, tingling wave spread over her body from that look, making all the tiny hairs on her arms stand on end.

"I'm still a man," he warned with that same low catch in his voice. "And you're extremely attractive to me."

She met his gaze evenly, although she wanted to shift once more under the surge of tension that was suddenly thick in the air.

He cleared his throat, all evidence of good humor gone as he looked away from her as if desperate for a distraction. "We are a territorial species and this is our land. The men who grabbed you don't belong in this area. Other Weres sometimes try to take over a territory. I suspect someone is thinking about starting a war with us. It's been done in the past and it'll keep happening. I think you were grabbed because they wanted to leave your body on our land so we'd find you and know we were being challenged. It's—" Jason shrugged, "a fucked-up thing some of my kind do."

"I don't want any part of your war."

"And I don't blame you. It's against our laws to drag humans into our world. Unfortunately not everyone follows the law. Just like humans, there are noble Weres and bad ones. Some who follow the rules and some who break them. Good. Evil. So that's why I think you were taken, why they brought you here, and why they wanted to kill you."

She let that information sink in. "I know you lied about the no phone to keep me from calling the police, but I need to call my friend Jenny. She'll be really worried. I understand why you don't want me to call the cops. They'd accuse me of being nuts anyway, wouldn't they? I mean, Werewolf stories have been around hundreds of years and everyone thinks they are pure fiction. No one would believe me. They'd want to drag me to a mental hospital if I started ranting about what really happened to me. I just want to go home."

He sighed deeply. "There's one of the four who chased you still unaccounted for and you saw the fifth wolf's face. He was probably their alpha. Their leader. You were taken from a gas station and if someone didn't see your abduction and report it as it happened, I'm certain someone has missed you by now. The police will be looking for you. This other pack also has your car. That means this asshole can find out who you are, what your name is, and where you live. He will kill you, Brandi. He has no choice. He has to protect his identity and his pack's secrets.

"Until we can figure out who this guy is and take him out, you aren't safe. Letting you make calls and allowing you to leave would mean helping this asshole find and kill you. Don't think your human laws will stop them. They can make your body disappear in ways you don't want to know about, but you have to trust that I won't let that happen. I didn't risk my life to save yours so you could die anyway. I want you to live. Calling your friend would put her in danger too. You don't want that, do you? You don't want to drag your friend into this war."

"I don't." The jolt of sickening fear made her feel physically ill when she thought about Jenny. "She's pregnant and engaged. We were going to spend the weekend together shopping for her wedding dress. They just found out about the baby and are planning on getting married before she starts to show. It sounds like a shotgun wedding, but they've been living together for two years. Their families are both thrilled. I was so excited for her…and now this happened. I hate for this to ruin such a happy time for her."

"That's why you need to stay here and not contact anyone until everything blows over. It's safer for them if they know nothing. Let my people handle this and when we get these asshole, you'll be free. It shouldn't take more than a couple of days. We'll come up with a cover story for you to tell everyone. Maybe someone grabbed you and then you got away in the woods. We'll say you got lost or something. We'll have time to think about it and come up with a good cover. I'll personally take you closer to the town of Dryer and drop you off in the woods next to the road. You can wave down someone for help and I'll follow you to make sure they take you to the cops. You just need to hang in there, Brandi. Let us find this evil asshole and protect you. We *will* find him. My people are out in the woods right now tracking where those bastards came from."

Jason seemed so heartfelt and sincere. His determination to protect her was more than endearing, enough to make her do something stupid—like believe him.

She nodded slowly, trying not to think about what happened to naive women who trusted the big bad wolf's good intentions. "All right."

He eyed her suspiciously, as if unsure of her determination to trust. "No more running away from me?"

"I'll stay."

Obviously satisfied, he stood and started to clear the table. Brandi hesitated and then decided the least she could do was help him. They did dishes side by side as the silence and the gravity of their situation hung heavily in the air. The handsome, massive man next to her washed the dishes while she dried them. He shot her a smile when they were done, and then turned to face her.

"My mother used to say many hands make light work. I forgot how true it is." His smile broadened, almost as if he was feeling nostalgic, but she thought she saw a tinge of sadness in his eyes when he confessed, "She's been gone for a long time. It probably sounds stupid to a human, missing my mother. I know humans are very, um…singular. They'll move clear across the country by themselves, but wolves like company. We stay close to our family and we need our pack for survival. We desire the companionship. Our lives sort of revolve around it."

"I understand. Humans aren't as singular as you think. We like companionship too." Brandi tucked a stray curl behind her ear, unable to believe the completely bizarre conversation she was having. "I also live alone. I know how hard it can be."

Jason was silent, studying her in a way that left her skin tingling as he let his gaze run over her, wearing nothing but his T-shirt. "Your ex was an idiot to let you go. That's a human thing. Wolves mate for life. We don't have divorces in our world."

"But you said your father left."

"He was human, and also an idiot," he reminded her. "Will you swear that you'll stay inside? I removed the phones. I want to trust you, but you don't know me and I don't know you. I need to go out there and help my people hunt this alpha son of a bitch down. We were supposed to have a run, but it's work now so the other wolves will be busy. You'll be safe inside the cabin." He gave her an apologetic look. "The SUV keys are leaving with me. There's no second set. It's a very long walk to a road and there are going to be a Weres out tonight. I'll be back in a few hours. Do you swear you'll stay here inside where you're safe?"

She nodded silently, not really trusting herself to say it out loud. It all felt too crazy to be real.

Jason walked out of the kitchen and Brandi followed him to the front door. She was trying not to breathe a sigh of relief, knowing he was leaving. This man — wolf — whatever he was, left her floundering. He was too broad and muscular, unbelievably tall and far too handsome for her sanity, and there was an honesty to him that resonated with her more than it should. The idea of him being so lonely bothered her. She just couldn't clear her thoughts and get a handle on the situation when he was giving her those looks that caused an ache between her legs she didn't want to have to acknowledge.

Jason turned the knob and glanced back to her. "You might want to stay away from the windows for the next few minutes. I'm going to be stripping. Please leave my jeans on the porch. I don't think you'd appreciate me having to come in naked. Unlike some of the movies, we can't shift with clothes on. They get tangled and make it difficult once we're in wolf form. Feel free to make yourself at home."

He shut the door before she could respond and she found herself staring at the aged wood in stunned disbelief.

Well, that didn't help my sanity!

Brandi hesitated for about two seconds before she ran to one of the windows.

She peeked out, barely moving the curtain. Jason's back was to her and she wasn't going to miss seeing him change. She needed confirmation that she wasn't going crazy.

He pulled his keys out of his pocket and tugged his jeans past his hips. He didn't wear underwear. She stared at his perfect backside. He had the nicest ass she'd ever seen on a man. He was tan all over, as if he spent a lot of time lying out in the sun naked, and it only added to his appeal. He shoved his jeans down his legs to reveal muscular thighs. She saw wounds on one of his legs. Bite marks. She knew they were from his fight earlier with the three wolves. They looked almost healed. She tore her gaze away from the scabbed gashes

He wasn't a hairy man. Some men had really hairy legs, but not Jason, which was surprising considering he was a part-time wolf. She swallowed, feeling guilty for a moment as she tried to remind herself she was just looking for confirmation that all this was real, rather than her being pervy and spying on him. She wasn't supposed to be checking him out, but the man had a hell of a body. It was hard not to appreciate it.

Jason dropped his keys on top of his jeans and crouched down. The change happened so fast, she blinked from the shock of it. In seconds he'd gone from skin to fur.

She was still trying to accept the massive black wolf was the same guy who'd helped her wash dishes as he grabbed his keys in his powerful jaws, leaped off the porch and raced off into the woods. He never looked back, and she stared at the pair of jeans laying on the bottom step once he was gone. That was all that was left of the man he'd been.

Brandi dropped the curtain, walked to the couch and sat down hard.

She wasn't losing her mind. Jason really was a Werewolf. She should be terrified of him but as she searched her emotions, it wasn't fear she found. It was fascination, an odd form of security she wasn't sure she should trust, and…desire.

Shock tore through her at the revelation. She was sexually attracted to the tall, dark-haired man with the mixed genes.

She looked around the cabin in a daze, unable to believe the one-eighty her life had taken in the past twenty-four hours. She'd woken up yesterday a sensible woman who was happy with her orderly, uneventful life. As boring as it was, she liked her career as a self-employed accountant with a sizable list of small-business clients. She enjoyed the freedom of working for herself and not answering to anyone. She'd made a bad choice once when she'd been younger and married Carl, but never again had she planned on falling for the wrong guy and giving up her self-worth.

Now Brandi was trapped inside a cabin in the woods and lusting after the big bad wolf.

Chapter Four

Jason headed straight into the woods without looking back, even though he had sensed Brandi's gaze on him the moment he walked out onto the porch. He tried not to think about her watching him change into one of the same creatures who'd nearly ripped her to shreds.

He tried even harder not to think about her reaction to him before he'd changed, because he'd caught it, even from outside—the unmistakable scent of female desire.

Wolves weren't known for restraint when it came to carnal things like the smell of female lust, but Jason was stronger than most. Perhaps it was his human genes that allowed him to exercise a little more sexual control, but his strength of will was paper-thin where Brandi was concerned. He was feeling *very* carnal, more so than he could remember being in a very long time. Perhaps ever.

But even more unnerving than the desire pumping through his blood stream, he was disturbed by how easy it was to expose himself to this woman. A human. He'd even discussed missing his mother. That was something he kept locked up tightly, since it was a weakness of sorts and wolves weren't known for making themselves vulnerable to strangers outside their pack. He didn't even talk with his alphas about it, though Desmon and Jazz were far more likely to understand than a human was. They'd suffered losses too, and more so, they were wolves.

His own kind.

Something that until this afternoon mattered more to him than anything else. He'd spent a lifetime denying any sort of connection to humans despite his father, or more likely because of him.

Not that the wolf in him was concerned with the not-so-minor complication of a lifetime of resentment directed toward the entire human race.

It took everything in Jason to focus on the job at hand and not turn back to do something more interesting than scavenging for the scent of rogue wolves in the woods. Jason wasn't sure what would've happened if Brandi's safety wasn't at stake. Something that probably would've shocked her more than she already had been, because he wanted to find the source of that female desire and claim it like the dirty dog he could be, but fortunately he also had the undeniable compulsion to eliminate this threat to her. It was more important to him than sex.

Even the wolf in him agreed, which was as unusual as everything else about his reaction to this human. The wolf was a wholly feral being, one whose needs were very simple — survival, serving the pack, fucking.

Not necessarily in that order, especially when a female smelled as sweet as Brandi Compro.

It would be another story if she were a wolf. He was feeling very protective of her even though she wasn't pack. That meant he might be very compatible with her, and typically he would explore that, and a female wolf would be just as willing to exchange sex and see if they were well-matched in more ways than one, but humans were wired differently.

Weres mated for life once they found the right one. In every case, a male Were existed to protect his mate. It circumvented all his other instincts, even that of his own survival. Jason wasn't real sure why he was feeling that way toward Brandi. Werewolf chemistry at its best. It happened all the time, but not with a human. At least not that often. There were wolves who'd decided to mate with humans. His mother was one, but look at how well *that* turned out and hers wasn't the only sad story he'd seen.

Deciding to focus on the issues in front of him, Jason leapt up the steps of a two-story cabin that was hidden in the densest, darkest part of the forest. It was even more secluded than Jason's cabin, and that was saying something.

He dropped his keys, changed forms and knocked on the door, finding himself winded in human form. He'd been running without even realizing it. He picked up his keys while he waited.

"Who is it?"

"I know you can smell me." Jason rolled his eyes at the sharp, predatory growl from the other side of the door. "It's Jason. Open up, Miles. I need your help."

"Fuck off!"

Jason shook his head, trying to hide a smile, because Miles would probably try to take his head off if he was looking through the peephole and saw it. As his closest neighbor, Jason considered it his duty to visit Miles at least a few times a week, and it always took some charm to get him to open the door.

"A rogue pack invaded the territory today…on our side of the woods." Jason didn't have the patience for charm this visit. "They attacked an innocent human female. They wanted to leave her mutilated body as a warning of an impending territory war."

Jason growled at the memory, his body suddenly tight with rage.

Miles opened the door. Bare-chested and barefoot, his long black hair hung past his broad shoulders. The deep, damaging scars that never stopped being painful to look at were clearly visible on his muscular chest and arms. His dark eyes were narrowed, his marred face contorted in fury. "Did they kill her?"

"No, she's back at my cabin. She's bruised up and scared, but she'll heal."

"What happened to the wolves who attacked?"

"They're dead." Jason voice was more wolf-like than human. "But their alpha got away, along with one of the other rogues. I intend to remedy that." Looking for a distraction to hide how deeply it bothered him that Brandi was hunted, Jason tossed his keys on one of the porch chairs. "I'm leaving them here while we hunt. I had to lock up my phones rather than risk her calling the police."

"She knows about us. What does Des have to say about that?"

Jason growled again. "The human's my problem. She's under my protection."

Miles's eyebrows shot up. For once the intense scowl he always wore eased to show genuine surprise. He leaned into Jason, sniffing curiously, obviously looking for the scent of sex. When Miles found nothing, he shrugged and said, "I'll get my rifle."

Jason changed forms without answering and headed back down the steps to wait. He preferred his wolf form. It made his thoughts clearer, less confused. In this state, he had one goal — eliminate the threat to Brandi because she smelled good and looked incredibly sexy wearing only his T-shirt and maybe, if he was very lucky, she'd let him find out if she tasted as good as she smelled.

"Pack politics aren't my problem. Neither is the human you're obviously sniffing after." Miles closed the door behind him. He hadn't bothered putting on any more clothes, but a 9mm was now tucked into his jeans. He clutched a semi-automatic rifle in his right hand. "But they're fucking with my side of the woods. That *is* my issue."

Miles couldn't change forms. The explosion that scarred him eight years before made it impossible. It had turned him into a lone wolf. He didn't need to shift to be nearly feral and savagely intimidating. A deadly shot. A vicious fighter. Miles was wild and unpredictable on his best days. With the exception of Desmon, Miles's cousin, most of the wolves in the pack avoided him out of fear.

He was just the guy Jason wanted on this mission. Miles wouldn't mind helping Jason kill a few wolves if they caught this alpha and the rest of his pack.

****

Brandi turned on lights as it grew dark outside.

She fed more logs into the fire to keep it going.

Wind hit the cabin. It sounded like a storm was approaching, from the way the gusts had picked up in the last hour, and she hugged her arms to her chest to fight her rising apprehension.

As crazy as it was, she had this unbelievable burst of energy that left her so on edge she was practically jumping out of her skin. She should be exhausted after spending all morning running for her life, but she felt as if she could sprint a hundred miles instead. Despite the chill in the air, she was sweaty, restless, making her feel as though she needed to be doing something—anything. She'd never been this jittery in her life.

Brandi rummaged through the cabin after Jason left and hadn't found a phone, just as he promised. She wasn't even sure why she'd looked, but she felt as though she needed to. It was as if there was a hole inside her she needed filled, so she opened drawers and looked in closets. Frantically. Even though she wasn't really sure what she was searching for.

There were four bedrooms upstairs. One had been turned into a gym. Jason liked to lift weights, and from the set of weights on the barbell, he could lift over three hundred pounds. One bedroom was storage. Another just held a twin bed and a dresser. The master had a king-size bed and a mahogany bedroom set. There were a few clothes on the floor. The room was obviously lived in, but like the rest of the home, it was mostly clean.

She walked to the window and peered out as she chewed on her bottom lip, still bursting with nervous energy. Maybe it was some sort of delayed adrenaline from the attack earlier.

Or maybe it was panic over Jason.

He'd been gone for about five hours. When was he going to return? She hadn't expected him to be gone that long and she wasn't sure why she needed him back so badly, but she did. She'd found the switch for the outside lamp as the sun had gone down. The porch was lit, but beyond the circle of light, there was only blackness.

It was so eerily quiet in the woods.

Except for the pounding wind, which wasn't helping her nerves.

Was Jason all right? Had he run into more of those evil Werewolves?

A violent gust shook the cabin again and she heard wood creak. Brandi shivered, but not from the cold. She was an independent woman who lived on her own and ran her own business, but she'd had a long day and tonight she was scared. Maybe that's where the energy came from. Fear. She wasn't so sure how she felt around Jason, but she felt safer when he was here and she wanted him to come back.

Needed it.

What if those men were looking for her and came to Jason's cabin?

Brandi suspected she was also working on a severe case of shock.

She hadn't found a weapon in the house. She'd looked after the quest for the phone turned up nothing. She'd even searched Jason's closet. The man had a lot of jeans and T-shirts. He also liked leather. He had two leather jackets, four pairs of leather pants, and three sets of leather boots in his closet.

No gun.

The windows quaked as the storm raged. She jerked toward the sound, her heart racing. Where the hell was Jason? She chewed on her lip once more, shocked she wasn't bleeding already. Nerves made her chew on her lip a hell of a lot. It felt swollen so she forced her teeth to release it and walked to the couch instead.

She sat down and stared at the fire sightlessly for a long while, before a howl tore through the night.

Brandi jumped from the metric ton of nerves flooding her system. It sounded close, so she stood up and turned toward the door expectantly.

Dear God, please let it be Jason.

Everything in her was wound tight, but something deep down told her things would be better once Jason was with her again. Maybe this hollow, aching feeling would stop.

She hugged her chest again—and then heard something on the porch.

She ran for the fireplace and grabbed up the fire poker just in case it *wasn't* Jason. She stared at the door before she heard another sound from outside.

Wood creaked, and it wasn't the wind this time.

She waited, her body a live wire of apprehension. If it was Jason, he would have to put on the jeans he'd left out there.

She saw the doorknob turn, but it held since she'd locked it. She slowly walked toward the door, waiting for Jason to call out to her and let her know it was him so she could unlock it.

Instead of Jason's voice, she heard something scrape the wood. She backed up as the knob turned again. Terror hit her hard as the door started to slowly ease open.

Then she forced herself to relax, remembering Jason had taken his keys with him.

Except, it wasn't Jason who walked in.

Brandi's breath caught in horror as she stared at the thin, tall man who stepped naked into the cabin. He was probably about twenty, with dark eyes and short brown hair. He stared at her in shock. A frown marred his forehead as he stood there gripping the handle of the door, before he sniffed the air curiously.

"Who are you?" Her voice shook.

His frown deepened. "That's *my* question. Who the hell are you?"

She backed up, clutching the fire poker like a baseball bat. "Jason isn't here."

"Good news for me." His gaze lowered to take in all of her as he let out a low whistle. "Nice legs. You wearing anything under there?" He shut the door behind him. "You're looking very tasty and you smell extra sweet. Jesus, you smell sweet."

"Leave. Now." Brandi gripped the weapon tighter despite her sweaty hands and reminded him once more, "Jason isn't here."

The man chuckled, as though walking into a house nude might be a normal situation for him.

"I heard you the first time. So where are you from, cutie? You're a short little thing with curves for miles. I've never seen a bitch like you, but I like it. Where did Jason pick you up? How long are you in the area?" He took a step toward her. "I don't smell Jason on you, so as far as I'm concerned, that makes you fair game. If he's out *there* when he has you in his house, he doesn't deserve you."

She kept her gaze on his face rather than acknowledge how very naked this stranger was. "Are you stupid? I said leave, asshole!"

"Why?" He glanced down at himself pointedly. "When I can think of better things to do."

She followed his gaze, seeing that he was aroused. She looked away, knowing she was in deep trouble as the man kept coming at her.

Brandi was officially sick of being stalked by crazy, naked wolf-men.

She swung hard, fearlessly, in a way she didn't think she was capable of, and nailed him with the fire poker in the gut.

He grunted loudly and doubled over, grabbing his stomach.

"You hit me!" His voice was a raspy growl. "Damn it. That—"

She hit him in the head with her second swing, blindsiding him to the point that he dropped to his hands and knees.

She dashed to the front door and flung it open without looking back. She ran outside, still gripping the fire poker. She wasn't going to be trapped in the cabin with a Werewolf she could've seriously injured.

Injured animals were dangerous.

She'd take her chances outside.

Another howl pierced the night as the wind continued to blow viciously. Brandi threw up her arm and closed her eyes as dust flew at her from the dirt road the SUV sat on. She let her hand drop and opened her eyes the second the wind died down.

She glanced around in the darkness, but couldn't make out much. The trees were just shadowy shapes in the pitch-black. She spun, facing the cabin, and saw the naked guy stumble outside. He was holding a hand to his bleeding head. He looked up and his eyes narrowed. He growled viciously at her, his teeth white and dangerously long in the night. The growl was deep and inhuman, which made it more of a terrifying sound coming from the man's throat. He dropped his hand and growled at her again.

"That was damn unfriendly. I see you need lessons on how to be nice." He stormed toward her. "If you like it kinky, you should've said so. You look a little fragile for rough sex but hell, with those legs and that body, I'm game to play."

Running into the woods was a bad idea. She couldn't see shit. She wondered if wolves had good night vision. *Probably.* She backed up and bumped the SUV. With nowhere else to go, because the woods were not an option—she'd done that enough for one day—she climbed up on the bumper, crawled to the hood and ended up on top of the roof. She could see thanks to the porch light as the man stared up at her in shock when he reached the SUV.

"Come down here. You'll dent Jason's ride and he's going to be pissed."

"Stay away from me!"

"I can't do that." The guy shook his head. "You're a little meaner than I'm used to, but you smell too fucking good. We're going to have to work something out."

She clutched the poker, feeling her hands shake.

Did these Werewolves miss that no-means-no part of health class?

"I'm not like you. I'm…" She swallowed hard. "Not like you. I don't grow a tail. Now shoo!" She waved her hand toward the woods. "Go chase a ball or something."

The man's mouth fell wide open and he gaped at her. He blinked more than a few times, and then slammed his mouth shut. "Did you really just tell me to go chase a ball?"

How stupid is this guy?

She frowned. Didn't he know his own kind? She was still wound up and more than a little irritable after the day from hell she was having, so she couldn't help but snap at this growling Werewolf, "Have you ever heard the term 'too stupid to live,' 'cause you could write the book on it, dumbass. I'm not a Werewolf, and I wouldn't be interested even if I were."

"That's it." The Werewolf stopped at the back of the SUV. "I'll pay for the dents myself when Jason freaks out." He jumped and the entire SUV moved when his weight hit the back bumper. "Lying bitch. I know you're a wolf. New bitches come into our territory looking for men to hook up with. What's a matter? Don't you think I'm good enough for you?"

Brandi screamed, almost sliding down the windshield when she heard a snarl. The Werewolf grabbed her, his grip steely and unbreakable despite his lanky frame. She screamed again as the fire poker was torn from her hand and tossed to the ground.

It started to rain, but she fought like her life depended on it, knowing she probably looked like a mad woman, kicking and screeching like she was.

"Son of a bitch," the man cursed while he fought to keep ahold of her. The rain fell harder, making her slippery as the fine coating of dust on her turned to mud. "If you don't stop, I'm going to play rough back and you won't like it!"

"Drop her." A low, inhuman growl cut through the raging storm, vibrating with a fury so potent it was almost tangible in the air. "Gently."

The man fighting with Brandi spun, holding her to him like a child clinging to a prize. Brandi saw Jason storming out of the woods totally naked. Her gaze locked with his just as he growled viciously and snarled, showing those sharp, deadly teeth in a way that made the other man look like a puppy.

"I said drop her gently, Paul. Be very careful or I will kill you."

"She took a fire poker to me, Jason. The bitch is in heat and she took a damn fire poker to me when I was just trying to help her out. What bitch turns down a perfectly good male when she's smelling like this? She's crazy!"

"You're treating a human under my protection like a bitch in heat?" Jason sounded completely incredulous, despite the inhuman rumble still heavy in his voice. "Please give me a reason to challenge you. Give me a reason to save this fucking pack from your stupidity!"

The growl he let out was deafening, his teeth seemed deadly as he jumped at the car like he couldn't help himself. Brandi and the other wolf nearly tumbled off the roof with how fast they both jerked back as Jason shouted, "She was in my house! Under my protection! That means she's mine! *And you touched her!"*

The other Werewolf, Paul, *did* fall off the roof with how quickly he let go of Brandi. She turned around, watching as he changed into a brown wolf before her eyes and took off running with a whimper she actually heard over the wind and rain.

Jason chased him, still human, still growling as though he was anything *but* human. He got all the way to the edge of the woods as the younger Werewolf slipped away. Then Jason yelled into the dense forage, "You better hide, you little shit! Stay out in these goddamn woods for the next three days 'cause I'm not forgetting. Hide like the rat you are. You go home to your mother and she will be watching me beat your ass! I'll make you cry in front of the whole pack!"

Brandi stood there on the roof as she watched Jason stalk back. Her hair was sticking to her neck, the shirt she was wearing clung to her body like a second skin, leaving very little to the imagination, but she was still wearing a whole hell of a lot more than Jason.

"I'm sorry," he whispered as he stopped in front of the SUV, buck-ass naked in the rain, to look up at her. "He's young and stupid. You're a beautiful woman, but I don't know why the fuck he thought a human was in heat. Rain and dust, I guess. It messes up our sense of smell. Must've been wishful thinking on his part." Jason's voice got a little husker as he tilted his head and eyed her legs. "This probably didn't help your shitty day."

"You think?" she asked dully.

Jason looked genuinely abashed. "Can I help you down?"

"How about putting on some pants first?" She looked to the porch. "The naked thing is a little distracting."

Brandi stayed on the vehicle, rain-soaked and miserable, with her heart still beating the hell out of her ribs. She was shaky in the aftermath, but she couldn't stop herself from watching as Jason bent over and picked up his jeans when he got to the porch.

She wasn't impressed with herself that she studied him, but she did.

That adrenaline she noticed earlier seemed to multiply a thousand fold as she admired that firm, muscular ass in the halo of the porch light before he tugged his jeans on, buttoned them and shoved the keys in his hand into his pocket.

She glanced away before he caught her staring at him, and folded her arms over her chest protectively. This day from hell had officially broken her, because she should not be standing there soaking wet in a strange man's T-shirt, lusting over him five minutes after almost being sexually assaulted.

"Are you ready to come down?"

Hearing his voice only made it worse. A shiver of raw, uncontained desire washed over her and she shook from the force of it, but said nothing. She crossed her arms tighter and refused to acknowledge him.

She didn't even trust her voice, that's how deeply he was affecting her.

After waiting hours for Jason to get home, needing him back to the point that she nearly ripped his cabin apart out of nerves. She couldn't speak to him, and she didn't dare look at him, because he would know. He'd know something about this day had made her crazy. She should not be shaking with desire like this after being chased...like a dog.

Again.

"I said I was sorry, Brandi." Jason waited as she stood there trying to get herself under control. "You're strong. Far more so than any other human I've met. Please don't choose now to break down."

She did have an impossibly difficult day; so much so, she wouldn't have been able to imagine it in her wildest nightmares. Brandi decided to give herself a little credit and admit, "I don't feel like myself. I'm shaky."

"Well, I guess so. Paul is very lucky I didn't fucking bury him for that stunt. If he wasn't so young, I would've. Young wolves, they still have puppy tendencies. They're not known for thinking before they jump." Jason's voice was still gruff, a little inhuman, but he sounded sincere again, like the man she remembered doing dishes with. "Come down and I'll make you a late dinner."

Jason reached out and caressed her bare ankle, sweeping this thumb over the back of it and she found herself leaning down before she made a conscious decision to do it. Jason took her hand and helped her climb off the SUV.

Brandi chalked it up to her shitty day when she let her guard down and wrapped her arms around him. She clung to him, feeling safer than she had in a long time.

Jason didn't hug her back. It felt as though his entire body tensed and every muscle was suddenly steel. The shock was icy cold, but her face was on fire despite the chill in the air.

Feeling completely mortified, she let him go. "I'm sorry. It's just...nerves."

She looked to Jason, who still hadn't said anything. Though it was dark, she was close enough to see how his eyes had dilated, unusually so, more animal-like than human, as if he was suddenly feral.

She couldn't help but ask, "Are you okay? Is this a wolf thing?"

"I…" Jason blinked, his voice was gruffer than ever as he looked down at her, and then shook his head in a very wolf-like manner. "Yeah. It's a wolf thing. We should go inside."

Considering it was still raining, Brandi had to agree.

Jason put his hand on the small of her back as the two of them walked to the cabin, and again she was unnerved by how comforting it was. She wasn't one to trust easily and she had to remind herself to guard her heart. Now more than ever, she should be careful. He wasn't even human.

Jason is more.

A Werewolf who'd saved her…twice.

And that didn't seem nearly as unnerving as it should.

Chapter Five

Jason was fucked.

Highly, irreversibly, and undeniably fucked on every single level.

Somehow, for reasons he couldn't begin to comprehend, Brandi was in heat.

No wonder Paul had chased her on top of the SUV. The scent of female pheromones was so strong, it overrode the fact that she was human. Paul was young, with very little control, and a female in heat could make any male go crazy. Jason was barely holding it together ever since he smelled what the rain and mud had hidden, until she wrapped her arms around him as if she was looking for more than a hug.

Everything in him was focused on breathing slow and steady through his mouth, but it wasn't working very well. Once they got inside the cabin, her scent was everywhere, drowning out all sense of reason. He could feel it sticking to his skin, sweet, feminine, making his dick hard and his mouth water. His canine teeth had grown long against his will, which was a first for him. He'd wanted women before. He'd been with females in heat, but this was different.

He wanted to bite Brandi.

Taste her.

Fuck her until they were both raw and aching.

The Werewolf chemistry that had created so many unions was working overtime on Jason, but she was human. He was fairly certain human males didn't claim their mates like wolves did and fuck them until they both passed out in complete exhaustion. Humans bought flowers and went out to dinner to court a relationship. They didn't sense a connection immediately and act on it like nature intended. They looked for all kinds of tiny clues and sorted through a million feelings before they hooked up, and eventually broke up after all that soul searching.

It had always seemed like a very slow and tedious process to Jason, but right now he would give anything to have taken more after his father. To be clueless like the humans, instead of feral and alert to sexual compatibility like the wolves, because he was more than aware of just how compatible he was with Brandi. She'd appealed to him since he'd first laid eyes on her, but now, it was clearly something much more carnal.

It was obvious she sensed it too. Even as a human, she had clung to him with an innate feminine instinct to be cared for and protected. He'd have to be blind to miss it.

Jason was half-human, it gave him a semblance of control, but even still, it was almost impossible to stop himself from going after her and letting nature take its course. His shirt was clinging to Brandi in all the right places, showing off the curves of her hips and clinging to her full tits that he wanted to lick, bite and suck on until she was writhing and begging under him.

"Are you sure you're okay?"

"Yeah, why?" he mumbled, still watching her wring out her long, curly hair. She was slightly bent over, putting her perfect, rounded ass on display. "Why wouldn't I be okay?"

Brandi looked at him with wide, innocent blue eyes, making him feel like the big bad wolf, plotting to get her into bed and ravage her after she'd been dealing with feral wolves all day.

"You growled."

"I did." Jason flinched, but he still couldn't look away.

"Is that another wolf thing?"

He nodded, still trying to breathe through his mouth. Still fighting to look away, but staring instead. "It's definitely a wolf thing."

"I'm freezing my ass off." She shivered as she straightened and obviously gave up on her hair. "You were gone a long time."

"Sorry." He flinched again, because it felt decidedly like he had failed to protect his mate, and that was a failure most male wolves couldn't tolerate. "We located the tracks where they parked the van they brought you in and we followed them to the road. They're gone. We didn't find your car and we didn't find any other wolves in the woods, either, but we're putting out more patrols. They might grab another human to kill and leave as a challenge for our territory. We're on alert. I had to talk to some of the other enforcers and it took some time."

Even as he fought against smelling Brandi, he couldn't help but notice the scent of blood. "You made Paul bleed?"

She glanced at the fireplace. "I hit him with the fire poker. It's outside. He threw it away after he grabbed me."

Jason arched an eyebrow, feeling himself tense for a different reason. Anything could've happened to her while dealing with a male wolf, even a young one, when she was in heat. "You thought you'd win against one of my kind with a fire poker?"

She hesitated. "It was the only weapon close to me. He had a key to your cabin. The door was locked. He unlocked it and walked in. Then he was naked and coming at me like..." She snapped her mouth shut. "What else could I do?

Jason slowly moved towards her. "Did he touch you, Brandi?"

Young or not, Paul was a dead wolf if he had done more than chase her.

She hesitated. "He just grabbed me, and then you came. Thank you for having wonderful timing. It seems you're very good at playing the superhero. Lucky for me. I was scared."

"I was on my way home and I heard you scream. You just made me run faster." He shuddered, trying not to think about what would've happened if he hadn't heard her. "Maybe you should take a shower. Warm up. I'll put more wood on the fire."

She nodded. "What about you?"

"I have a shower in my room."

"Won't we run out of hot water?"

He couldn't help but snort, because he planned on taking the coldest, most miserably icy shower possible. "No, we're good. Use all the hot water you want, darlin'."

****

Jason thought Brandi taking a shower would give him a reprieve, but her scent was still everywhere, making every muscle in his body tighten. He threw some logs on the fire, and then went to the SUV to get his phone out of the lockbox under the passenger seat where he'd stored it.

Even outside, in the rain, Jason couldn't stop smelling her desire now that he knew it was there. So he got in the vehicle and called one of his alphas, looking for guidance.

"What's going on?" Desmon answered on the first ring, his voice tense like it got when they knew another pack was trying to move in on their territory. "I better not hear you say it's bad news."

"It's bad news."

"Un-fucking-believable." Desmon groaned. "Why don't they just leave us alone? We don't even know these goddamn wolves."

"'Cause we've earned the reputation for being the hardest pack to take down in Northern California. We're a small pack, but we're strong. The power play is massive. Plus, we have two alphas. That's twice the challenge, and—"

"Thank you, Jason. It was a rhetorical question. I wasn't actually looking for a response. I know the issues, I'm just irritated by them. What it is about wolves? They always have to go and piss in someone else's territory to prove their dicks are bigger. Like sharing a border with Goodwins isn't bad enough."

"Sorry, it was just easier to worry about your problems than my own." Jason shook his head as he said it. "Somehow I put her in heat. I'm so fucked, Des."

"The human?" Desmon sounded as shocked as Jason felt. "What the hell did you do to her?"

"Nothing." Jason shrugged "She was injured. It wasn't major, just a small head wound. I licked it, but—"

"A human let you lick her head?"

Jason ran a hand through his wet hair. "She was asleep. I thought I'd help her heal."

Desmon was quiet for a moment. "Were you bleeding at the time? Is it possible that your blood mingled with hers?"

"I had a cut on my lip."

"Damn it, Jason. You're half human. Didn't you think about how mixing your blood with hers might cause a reaction? Let me guess. You were turned on at the time?"

Jason winced as he admitted, "Yes."

"Wow, you *are* fucked." Desmon snorted. "Half the pack's out protecting the borders with Jazz. They'll be out for the next couple days, and you're going to have a lot of company unless you find a way to cool her off."

"She's already traumatized," Jason reminded him. "She was nearly killed by Weres. It's been a really bad fucking day for her."

"She'll have a worse day if she ends up with a houseful of unmated males wanting to fuck her. Not to mention, leaving a woman to deal with a blood-induced heat is cruel. It's agonizing for them. I know you don't like humans. I can take care of her if you have an issue. I've been with human women. I can be gentle."

Jason growled. Even though Desmon was his alpha, he couldn't help the viciousness of his wolf that wanted to rip his friend apart for that suggestion.

Low and threatening, he snapped, "Don't even *think* about touching her."

"Okay." Desmon sounded unimpressed. "Go take care of it then, big wolf, if you're so fucking territorial."

"Fine." Jason was about to hang up, thinking that Desmon had offered less than zero help.

Then Desmon interrupted him. "And I better not hear about you kicking the shit out of any young wolves just because you decided to share blood with a human against her will. We all know horny pups turn into idiots when they're thinking with their dicks, and you've got a temper. One of them will step out of line, it's a given if she's in heat, and you'd punish them. Then I'll have their mothers knocking down my door because of your fuck-up."

"It was an accident." Jason's voice was still low and inhuman.

"I don't care. You might want to forget you're half human, but it's fact. Your blood mingling with a straight human's when you're turned on can cause side effects. It could happen to any wolf with enough blood, but she's obviously more sensitive to yours. Either take care of her, or call me, but I don't want any fights over her. We have enough problems."

Desmon hung up on him. Jason looked at his phone, groaned, and then dropped his head back against the seat, wondering how the hell he was going to explain to Brandi what he'd accidently done to her.

****

Brandi showered until the water turned lukewarm, which made her a bitch when Jason needed the hot water too, but she was just so uncomfortable. The truth was, she was sexually frustrated, which seemed insane, but Jason was *not* hard on the eyes. Not at all.

She was so pent-up and aching with need, she ended up touching herself. With her hand against the shower wall, she rubbed her clit, feeling the water beat against her back. Then she fingered herself, and closed her eyes, imagining it was Jason inside her, his breath hot against the back of her neck. She could almost hear his voice, a little gruff, a little inhuman, and she came faster than she had in her entire life.

The orgasm hit so hard she practically fell to her knees from the force of it.

It helped the ache for about twenty seconds, then the longing seemed to get worse, more demanding, until she found herself doing it again.

And again.

Each time the need got more overwhelming, until she couldn't think about anything but Jason, and the way his eyes had dilated when they were outside. It turned her on to think about him looking at her like that. Seeing the way his pupils went wide triggered something so sexual, it was fully unnamable for her.

It was little wonder when the hot water finally ran out.

Unfortunately, she was too sensitive to stay in the shower once it turned cold, so she got out and grabbed a towel off the sink. Her hands were shaking, and she would've assumed it was from the cold, but her skin felt unnaturally warm. She was sweating, though she just got out of a shower, and being dripping wet wasn't helping anything.

She dried off quickly, and then stood there in a towel as she tied her hair up, wrapping it in a knot since she didn't have anything to make a ponytail with. She was just pulling the ends through the top of the bun when a low growl made her turn toward the locked door.

Brandi should've been scared, considering how many times she'd been growled at and chased by Werewolves today, but instead goose bumps spread over her arms for an entirely different reason. The lust that forced her to touch herself until the water ran cold slammed back into her, a million times stronger than it had been before, making her forget about being sweaty, sticky and uncomfortable.

She blinked heavy-lidded eyes, the world almost hazy from the force of sensation that washed over her. The bathroom was steamy, making even her reflection dim, and it had her wondering if her vision was blurry. At the same time she felt hyper aware of other senses. She could hear breathing on the other side of the door. Raspy, uneven, more than a little primal, and again, she should be frightened.

But she knew it was Jason.

Brandi wasn't real sure how she knew, but she did, and more so, there was some sixth sense that told her Jason wasn't a danger. At least not the chase-her-and-eat-her kind of danger. His brand of danger felt good, especially when she could smell him like she could. His scent wrapped around her like the steam, heavy in the air, all warm and spicy, making her feel safe in some ways and completely wild in others. She approached the door, and unlocked it, still turned on and thinking about him as she put her hand on the handle.

"Don't open the door. Not yet." Jason's voice was gruffer than it had been outside in the rain, not quite human, just how she'd imagined when she touched herself. "We have a problem."

Brandi had her fill of problems for one lifetime, but that sixth sense was in higher gear. Nothing that smelled as good as Jason did right now could be evil. His scent was so potent she could almost taste it on her tongue. Still, she released the handle and went back to the counter.

All she could do was ask, "What?" as her mouth watered and her pussy throbbed. She could physically feel the pulse of need between her legs when the icy-hot rush of lust sent an electric tingle into her fingertips.

Jason growled again, this time louder, more territorial as he grunted, "Christ, your scent. I can almost taste you on my tongue."

She sucked in a surprised gasp.

"I was just thinking the same thing. Why?" Brandi closed her eyes, remembering the way he looked without his shirt on, his broad chest, his thick, muscular arms, that tattoo that was more like a warning than decoration. Her voice became a little softer, a little wispier with longing. "Why do you smell so good?"

She could hear him touch the other side of the door, like a caress. It wasn't a forceful touch, but she could still sense it as he said, "You do too. Fuck, do you smell good. You have no idea."

"I c-can hear things I shouldn't," she mumbled, still trying to think past the sexy aroma that was fogging her senses and the sexual need that was making her knees weak. "It's like everything is amplified. I feel like my vision is off, but everything else is too sharp."

"It's the steam. Your vision's sharper too, just like your sense of smell. Brandi, I did something by accident." He paused, like he didn't want to admit it. "I, um…" Jason groaned, still sounding miserable. "Sometimes when my people get hurt, we'll lick the wound to help it heal."

"Like a dog," she said before she could stop herself.

"Yeah," he whispered. "Like a dog. Our saliva is healing. It's not a big deal. We can lick a human. We don't have diseases like your people do. It'll just help the wound heal faster. If you look in the mirror, you'll notice the cut on your forehead is almost gone."

Brandi rubbed at the fogged-over mirror, and leaned in, seeing that it was nearly healed. Even the green tinge of bruising she'd noticed earlier was gone and she touched the pink scar in shock. "Oh my God."

"I didn't like seeing you bleeding. It upset me to see you hurt and I wanted it healed. It was an instinct I should've stopped. I should've thought clearer. Our saliva only heals, but I had a cut on my lip and our blood can be sort of contagious in certain situations. It's a little more dangerous."

Brandi turned to look at the door, hearing his breathing on the other side more clearly than she should. "Did you make me a Werewolf?"

"No. It would take a lot more blood than a few drops from one small cut on my lip, but it has other effects. They're temporary. It really shouldn't have happened at all, except I'm…very attracted to you. That's a deciding factor, and our chemistry must've triggered something." He groaned again like he couldn't help it. "Holy shit, you smell good."

The way he said it was like having a liquid aphrodisiac injected into her veins, but still Brandi stared at the door and asked, "What'd it trigger?"

"We're animals. We're very susceptible to natural chemistry. Sometimes the exchange of blood can cause a woman to go into heat. Even a human woman. It obviously took longer because the amount was so small. It shouldn't have affected you at all, but like I said, I was attracted to you. I wasn't mindless with lust or anything, but I wanted you.

Clearly, my blood triggered something. You're in heat. Like a bitch goes into heat. You're putting out pheromones wolves can smell a mile away."

"Other wolves?" she asked as fear finally made its way past the attraction to Jason clouding her thinking. "Are they going to attack me?"

"I wouldn't let them do that." Jason was easy to believe when his voice got so low and dangerous like that. "I'd beat the shit out of them first, but for obvious reasons, injuring a bunch of young, dumb males trying to get with a human I accidently put into heat would seriously piss off my alpha."

"You have an alpha?" Brandi asked in disbelief. "There's someone bigger than you?"

"Yes, I do." Jason sounded grim. "And Desmon's extremely pissed off at me right now. Our pack is unique. We actually have two alphas. I'm sure as soon as Jazz gets back, he's going to be pissed too."

Oh great!

Brandi was silent as she stood there feeling so hot and frustrated she could hardly think straight. More than anything, she was fighting the instinct to open the door, which seemed crazy, but…

"I could help you," Jason cut into her thoughts. "If you wanted me to. I know you're probably very frustrated."

She snorted at that understatement.

"I'm not forcing anything. I'll fight to protect you and you can stay in there, but if we hooked up, your scent would change and it'd solve a lot of problems for both of us. You'd still be in heat, you'd be putting off pheromones, but they'd be different. It's hard to explain, but it, um…you'd smell sort of claimed. It's nature's way of keeping us from killing each other."

"Claimed?" Brandi repeated.

"Yeah," Jason agreed, his voice still gruff, with that uneven breathing. "You'd smell like that because it'd be mixed with my scent. They'd know I was…"

"Claiming me," Brandi finished for him. "Is that what you want? You want to claim me, Jason?"

"I want to claim the fuck out of you, Brandi," Jason assured her in a way that caused a fresh sheen of goose bumps to spread over her arms. "I want to claim you until neither of us can see straight."

Brandi shifted where she stood and it was likely he could smell how his words made her feel, because he growled again. Loudly. She wished his voice didn't affect her like it did, that it didn't make her needy. Worse, she felt like his scent was wiping out all sense of self-preservation.

Still, he didn't knock down the door. He didn't even demand she open it, even though his need was still masculine and tangy on her tongue, making a very vain, feminine part of her she'd never once tapped into until now savor it.

Then the long, scary sound of a wolf howl broke the air. She turned towards the window, hearing it in the distance. She shuddered, just as another howl broke through the night.

A different howl.

This one was much closer. More intimidating. Vibrating with warning, and Brandi didn't even stop to think before she reached for the doorknob.

She was nothing if not a survivor, and she may not know much about Jason, but she knew she felt safer with *him* than she did with any other wolf she'd met.

She turned the knob, but Jason was the one who pushed the door open, as if one more second would've been too long. Then he was standing there shirtless, impossibly broad, muscular, with those dark, primal eyes dilated like a hungry animal's and she should've turned and ran the other way.

She reached for him instead, touching the fire, knowing she'd probably get burned as she threaded her fingers into his dark hair and pulled him to her. If there was a high like having a buff, sexy, incredibly deadly Werewolf curve into her hold like she owned him, Brandi couldn't even remotely fathom it.

The way Jason bent down and licked at the curve of her neck, when she forced him there for reasons she didn't fully understand, nearly knocked her to her knees from the explosion of lust that filled her. His scent drowned her. The caress of his low groan against her sensitive skin made her feel as though she were going to climax right there. She shuddered from the way he dragged his tongue slowly up the curve of her neck to her ear.

Brandi accepted him, holding him to her as he reached for the knot in the towel between her breasts and pulled it undone.

He tossed the towel aside, leaving her naked and exposed when she'd never been comfortable nude in front of a man after her ex-husband's verbal abuse. It was an instinct deeper than whatever Jason's blood did to her that had her trying to step away, but Jason wouldn't let her go now that she'd opened the door.

He grabbed her hips instead, pulling her tight against him, letting her feel the outline of his hard cock through his jeans. Something about his hold was impossible to push away from, so she hid by turning her head, refusing to look at him as he stared down at her naked body.

Jason seemed to take it as an invitation, and licked her neck again. He nipped at her shoulder, with teeth a little too long to be human. She thought she felt the prick of broken skin and turned back against her will, watching as he dragged his tongue slowly over the small blossom of blood on her pale skin. His eyes were closed, dark eyelashes like half-moons on his cheeks, and the sound he made as he tasted her blood was so purely indulgent, she found herself wanting to see him bite her again just to hear it once more.

Then he dropped to his knees on the bathroom floor and sucked on her tits, taking a nipple into his mouth with the flash of long canine teeth.

Rather than be afraid, she ran her fingers through his short hair, pushing it off his forehead so she could see him better. She wanted to watch him worship her, because that's exactly what it felt like as she completely forgot about being embarrassed…and let herself be claimed instead.

Chapter Six

Brandi was so smooth.

All over.

Silky-soft skin that smelled so fucking good it was taking everything in Jason not to bite her. He could still taste her blood on his tongue from that nip on her shoulder and it was driving him crazy.

He was hungry for her in a way he'd never experienced before. This wasn't sex. This was need. An aching addiction he wasn't prepared for, and his hands shook as he fought to rein himself in.

He tried to hide his canine teeth from her as he moved over and sucked on her other nipple, but she was watching him, which in and of itself was hot as hell.

Then she whispered, "Your teeth. Are you going to change into a wolf again?"

He shook his head and looked up at her. "No. I just feel very…" He wanted to tell her how carnal he felt—primal and desperate—but he didn't. Instead he grabbed her hip with one hand and fanned a thumb over her tightened nipple. "Possessive," he whispered. "It makes me want to taste you. To drown myself in you. I've never been with a woman like you before."

"A human?" she asked curiously.

"That too," he agreed, but that wasn't what he meant.

Brandi was so soft and welcoming when she should be terrified. Bitches were notoriously aggressive. Life made them such, and that's how most male wolves liked them, but maybe Jason was more human than he realized because feeling Brandi's timid fingers in his hair and smelling her desire was almost too much.

"You're very beautiful. Very sweet." He used his hold on her hip to force her down a little and bit her other shoulder lightly, just enough to taste. She let him though her small gasp told him she felt it. "So fucking sweet."

He leaned down and pressed a kiss to her hipbone and ran both hands over her curvy hips once more. Then he decided to taste what was really driving him wild, making him feel more wolf-like than anything, despite his promises to the contrary.

"I need you in my bed," he decided, wanting to see her spread out on his sheets, covered in his scent.

He stood and scooped Brandi up.

She let out a screech and shoved at his shoulder. "You have to stop doing that! You'll drop me!"

"Have I once hurt you, Brandi? Have I done anything but try to keep you safe?" He couldn't hide the insult in his voice. "Werewolves are stronger than humans. We're more agile and coordinated too."

She took a shuddering breath and grew pliant in his arms. When he walked to his bedroom door and kicked it open, she snaked one arm up around his neck. She felt soft again, welcoming and accepting, hazing out his thoughts and washing away the insult.

"This isn't something I thought I'd ever have," she whispered as she curled into him. "Thank you."

"Your husband," he said knowingly as he laid her down on his bed. "He didn't appreciate you."

She shrugged and looked away rather than answer.

"He didn't take care of you like he should have." He crawled over her, his overactive senses hearing the quickening of her breathing and the rapid thump of her heartbeat. "If I was your mate, I'd savor you. I'd taste you every day. I'd fuck you so often you'd never stop feeling me."

She let him suck on her tits again and didn't complain when he bit her softly. Brandi indulged him, because he was starting to learn she was that type of person, gentle, loving and giving.

He moved down her body, kissing, licking, while using every ounce of self-control he had not to bite her. It scared him, the need he had to sink his teeth into her and own her completely.

Mated Werewolves bit each other.

They exchanged blood to deepen their bond.

He decided not to think about it too hard.

Brandi was in his bed, so open and trusting, smelling sweetly of female need, and he wouldn't be a man if he didn't give in to the indulgence and spread her thighs. He looked down to admire the smooth feminine lines of her pussy that was hairless, something he'd never seen on a woman before.

It turned him on like crazy.

He didn't ask, he simply took what was in front of him, licking the full length of her pussy with a low growl as he savored her taste on his tongue. Brandi cried out and fisted his hair. She was ripe for fucking, and the sounds she made as he licked and sucked her clit drove him wild. She was so responsive. It was easy to push her over the edge. Her thighs shook, her fingers tightened in his hair, and then she was pitching beneath him with a shuddering gasp that made Jason's cock twitch with desperation.

"God," she panted, her thighs still shaking. "I think I needed that. I've had the worst day ever until you. Thank you."

The idea of how differently this day could've ended made Jason tense with fury. He wished he could go back and kill those wolves who'd hunted her all over again. He thought about the other two still out there somewhere and he couldn't hide the low, furious growl.

She tugged his hair, forcing him to look up at her, and Jason said, "I'm thinking of the ones who hurt you," rather than admit he was plotting the long, agonizing death of the ones still left. "You make me feel protective."

"That makes sense," she whispered as she stroked the damp strands of hair off his forehead and looked at him.

"Since I feel very protected when I'm around you. That was amazing."

It was likely Brandi didn't know how deeply her words were going to resonate with the wolf in him. A bitch wouldn't just let a male assert the right to protect her, not when wolves were as territorial as they were, and it felt like the final nail in the coffin.

Jason lost the tight hold he had on his carnal side as he leaned down and kissed her, hard, forgetting she was human as he took advantage of her gasp of surprise. He pushed his tongue past her parted lips, tasting her, savoring the way she became languid under him. Brandi let him take her mouth like he wanted to take her body, wholly, on the razor's edge of rough as he grabbed her ass and forced her tightly against him.

It made them both mindless. He ripped at the button to his jeans as the scent of female pheromones nearly choked the air out of the room. He wanted to feel her bare skin against his. When he finally kicked off his jeans, she wrapped her legs around him, every bit as greedy as Jason.

It was too much to resist. The tight-hold Jason had on the wolf sprang free and he took her with one hard thrust—wild and possessive—the way he would take a bitch instead of his soft and kind Brandi. It was driven all the more by the way she moaned and arched into him, surrendering to the pleasure, smelling like lust as she wrapped her arms around his back and held on to him.

She rode out the passion with him, meeting him thrust for thrust, until they were both sweaty and primal. Their lips brushed in hard, breathless kisses. She swallowed his low grunts and growls as the ecstasy started washing over Jason to the point he lost all control of his urges.

Maybe that's why he mated her.

His climax was a few shallow thrusts away, leaving him so animalistic he didn't stop to think before he let his fangs grow long and partially shifted while inside her. He bit her without thought, and he wasn't gentle either. He sank his teeth in deep, right at the tender spot in the curve of her neck.

If he hurt her, he couldn't tell, because the bliss of their bonding was all-consuming. Her nails were sharp in his shoulders as she gave in to the pleasure and climaxed beneath him.

She peaked so hard he could feel her pussy clutching at his dick as he took her over and over again, until he had no choice but to follow her. He came violently, and grabbed her ass, holding her tighter against him when his dick pulsed and swelled inside her.

She gasped and shuddered beneath him while he shifted back. The change had been subtle, his fangs, a little more hair, and he knew she didn't notice. His body was shuddering from the pleasure. He couldn't talk. He could barely ease the tight hold his teeth had on her neck. When he did, he licked the wound and pressed fervent kisses against her shoulder because the bliss was still vibrant for both of them.

"God, Jason, that feels good." She sighed and ran her fingers over his sweaty shoulders. Her pussy clenched around his dick, making it obvious it was the way he swelled inside her that she was enjoying. "It makes it last and last. I've never felt anything like that. I just kept coming and coming."

It took several long minutes before he could pull out of her, and during that time, she became lax beneath him, stroking her hands down the length of his back in a way that could become addicting. He liked the way Brandi petted him and he wanted to lay there all night enjoying it.

Unfortunately, reality smacked him in the face and the icy dread nearly choked the breath out of Jason's chest.

"Are you okay?" Brandi asked when he stiffened from the fear. He rolled away from her rather than answer. She sat up and ran her hand down his back once more in that addicting way he liked so much. "Jason?"

He forced himself to breathe, knowing he didn't want to have this discussion when she was in the height of a heat. He turned back to her, seeing that she still had blood on her shoulder, running down the curve of her left tit, and on instinct he found himself leaning into her and licking the stain clean. He sucked on her nipple, still puckered and tight with arousal, and then moved up to her shoulder.

She fell back against the bed, and he crawled over her, needing to be close. He used his thumb to caress her bottom lip before he leaned down and kissed her. It wasn't the same hard, bruising kiss from earlier. It was a little more loving, and Brandi opened to him as she had before, letting him slip his tongue past her lips and savor her.

When they finally parted for air she was panting, smelling of lust once more, and he just gave in and buried his face in her neck. He licked the wound before he kissed the tender spot, feeding her need until she was the one wrapping her thighs around him, forcing him in, begging breathlessly, "Just once more."

So Jason took her rather than think about the fact that he had just mated Brandi, tying her to him for life — without her knowing it.

Chapter Seven

Brandi couldn't stop wanting Jason.

The need didn't give in to exhaustion like it normally would. It calmed for a bit, and then built once again until she found herself under Jason, her nails dragging down his back as she arched and climaxed more violently than she had in her entire life.

That wasn't even the craziest part.

She couldn't seem to stop touching him, craving him near and feeling bereft when he left. Like when one of them snuck off to the bathroom or the time he went downstairs to get them a snack. Each time felt like an eternity. Even as the streaks of early morning pink filtered in through the window, she wanted him close.

She was probably losing her mind, but there were worse ways for it to go.

When Brandi decided on a desperately needed shower, Jason followed, and she was glad to let him. It seemed like Jason hated the separation as much as she did.

So that's how she ended up in his small shower, with Jason's big, strong body taking up most of the space. Neither of them minded. Instead, Brandi moaned when Jason wrapped his arms around her from behind and buried his face in the curve of her neck. The scent of soap was still heavy in the air, mixing with the overwhelming aroma of male lust.

She wasn't even sure how she knew it was Jason's desire she smelled, but she did, and she loved it more than anything in the world. She grabbed his wrists, admiring how thick they were, and held him closer as she said, "Touch me. Just one more time."

"Every time is just one more time," he chuckled against the shell of her ear. "Greedy."

"I'm sorry," she panted. "I just can't stop wanting you."

"Never apologize for that." He moved his lips down to the curve of her neck and licked the small wound he'd caused with his teeth their first time. "I'll give you anything you want. All you have to do is ask."

He kept kissing her neck as he slid his hands lower, caressing her stomach before clutching her hip. It seemed like a million years ago that she thought to be ashamed of her body in front of this man, but it'd only been one night.

One incredible, magical night that she wanted to last forever.

When he slid his fingers between the folds of her pussy, she spread her legs for him and tossed her head back against his shoulder. He growled in that low, possessive way that made her nipples tighten.

It was so easy to surrender to him.

Too easy.

Right then, she didn't care about how bold she was being for this Werewolf. Brandi placed her arms against the shower wall and let him hold her and finger-fuck her until her low moans resonated over the hum of the water hitting the shower tiles.

"Come for me, darlin'," he demanded against the sensitive skin of her neck, his voice low and dominant. "When I want to hear you, you let me hear you, don't you?"

Damn if she didn't do what he told her to.

She came hard, letting herself be loud because she knew he wanted to hear it. It felt good to scream like that, to give in to the pleasure rushing over her and not hold back.

Brandi was still vibrating from her orgasm when he turned her around. Jason lifted her up, forcing her to wrap her legs around his waist. His hands were shaking, making it obvious his control was slipping.

"I need inside you," he grunted, his hard cock sliding against her opening. "Just one more time, okay?"

She nodded, and dipped her head to hide her smile from just how closely his words mirrored hers. She curled around him, arms tight on his broad shoulders, feet hooked together at the small of his back, and she trusted him completely not to drop her when the thick head of his cock breached her.

She gasped from the feeling, so full, the bliss seemed to swallow her whole. He pushed in deeper, warm and decadent, pulling her down until all she could feel was Jason.

"Fuck, you feel good," he grunted as he bottomed out in her, and just held them both there like he was savoring it. "Best I ever felt in my life. No lie, the fucking best."

"Yeah?" She pulled back to look at him, knowing she was making herself vulnerable as she whispered, "I don't believe it."

"Yes, you do." He smiled, as if the statement was ridiculous. Then he pulled out halfway and thrust in, hard, making her gasp again. "You know we're amazing together."

She hid her face in that safe space between his neck and shoulder rather than respond. Her feelings were suddenly all over the place. It was easier just to feel him and stop thinking about the rest. His strokes were shallow, the friction of it over and over again making the pleasure burn brighter, but it was teasing too. Brandi was tired of being teased. She dug her nails into his shoulder, letting him know she needed more, wanted it hard and fast like the times before.

She was on the edge of begging when he bit her shoulder lightly and growled, "Tell me."

"Tell you what?" she gasped when he took her a little harder. Then she pushed her hips back against his in a silent plea for more. "God, what do you want to hear?"

"I want to hear it's the best. *That we're the best.* I want you to admit it doesn't get any fucking better than it is right now."

Brandi understood now why Jason had smiled earlier at her show of insecurity when she hadn't believed him. Without a doubt, this was the most incredible sex she had ever had in her life — by a long shot.

There's no way it could get any better, so she said, "It's the best," and then bit at his neck, not knowing why she wanted to break the skin with her teeth. "It's amazing. *You're amazing.*"

She did it then, bit him hard enough to taste the copper tang of blood against her tongue. Why did he taste *so* good? Why did she like it? She was struck with the urge to taste him over and over again.

Luckily, Jason didn't seem to mind.

His growl was undeniable as he started thrusting harder, faster, deeper, leaving her breathless and moaning. She was tinkering right on the edge, anxious to fall over. She was clawing at his back in her desperation when he returned the favor and bit her back, sinking his teeth in deep, and like before, the electric shock of pleasure shattered her. The ecstasy was white-hot, searing through her, stealing her breath, and from somewhere that seemed very far away, she heard a shout of female pleasure she vaguely recognized as her own.

It was that all-encompassing.

Jason followed her, thrusting hard one last time before he stiffened. She could feel his cock throbbing deep inside her, locking them together and extending their orgasms for what seemed like forever.

It took a long time for Brandi to feel as though she was coming back to earth, but she started to notice for the first time how heavy her arms and legs felt. As if the lust fueled rollercoaster ride she'd been on since Jason accidently put her into heat was slowly pulling into the station.

"God," she whispered against his skin, licking his neck once because she couldn't resist and finding it salty with a fresh sheen of sweat. "Sleepy."

"I bet." He traced his fingers up the line of her spine in a gentle caress. "I think we finally exhausted that heat of yours."

"Yeah," she agreed softly.

It was all she could think to say. She didn't realize how much raw adrenaline was pumping through her until it all fell out of her at once. She couldn't keep her eyes open if she tried. Brandi just cuddled against Jason, with him still inside her, all warm and still pulsing a little.

Brandi never felt him pull out.

She fell asleep instead.

****

Brandi stayed asleep as Jason carried her out of the shower, and took the time to dry her dewy skin and tuck her under the covers. Then he sat next to her on his bed, admiring the way she looked there.

He'd heard about matings and the overwhelming feelings they could cause, even if they happened unexpectedly between two strangers, but he hadn't anticipated it being this strong. Looking at this fragile woman in his bed was almost terrifying, because he realized what he would turn into if something happened to her.

A murderous demon, like something out of a horror movie.

He stroked her wet, curly hair away from her face, admiring her beautiful features. They had to do something more to protect her. To make her less delicate. He could turn her, but he knew that was something they would have to deal with much later. That was if she didn't freak out and leave him when she found out he'd bound them together without her permission.

He hadn't meant for it to happen. He honestly didn't need the complication, especially after he'd spent a lifetime dealing with repressed anger at humans after his father left.

The bastard could've stayed.

Jason's mother could've changed him into a wolf, but his father's pride got in the way. He couldn't deal with the other males in the pack being more powerful and intimidating than him. His father may never have been as strong as other Werewolves if Jason's mother changed him, but it would've been enough for his father to survive. Their pack had been wild and primitive back in those days before Desmon and Jazz took over, but many would've accepted him. They had others who'd been born human and turned later. Not every wolf was supposed to be an enforcer like Jason. They had tradesmen. Plumbers. Electricians. Subcontractors who went off to college with the humans and learned what they needed to help their pack. They had wolves who helped Desmon with taxes instead of guard the borders like Jason.

Instead his father left, and Jason had a lifetime of fury built up in regards to humans, but he still couldn't regret mating Brandi. Something about her struck such a deep cord in him. The only thing he found himself doing as he sat there, still caressing the wet hair at her temples, was plotting ways to keep her exactly where she was now, in the cabin, in his bed, content and sated from too much sex.

His whole world had just been turned upside down by this soft, gorgeous human, because keeping her suddenly became the only thing in the world that mattered to him.

easily be perceived as a high-powered, bad-boy business executive in the human world.

Impossibly tall and broad, the Werewolf leaned against the counter in a finely tailored gray suit instead of wearing jeans and T-shirts like all of the other Werewolves she'd met. He had long midnight-black hair that he'd tied back. If he were human, Brandi would think he was Native American. Tan, with a strong jaw line, but he had piercing blue eyes that were almost off putting. She couldn't look away from him, especially when he took a long drink from the coffee cup in his hand and arched an eyebrow curiously at her.

"Brandi, this is my alpha, Desmon Nightwind." Jason was sitting at the table, still looking like a very grumpy Werewolf as he gestured to the long-haired man. "Desmon, Brandi."

"Hello, Brandi." Desmon's voice was low, commanding, like that of an incredibly powerful man used to being obeyed. "I hear you've had a bad few days."

It wasn't hard to understand why he was the alpha.

"I, um…" She hesitated, feeling unnerved as she looked back to Jason. Worried he might be in trouble, she shook her head. "It started bad, but it improved. Jason's been very kind."

"Kind?" Desmon said with an edge of sarcasm in his voice. "Is that what we're calling it?"

"Is there some sort of rule against humans and Werewolves having sex?" Brandi asked, feeling brave in the face of this intimidating Werewolf.

She didn't want Jason to get into trouble. It was obvious Desmon could smell what happened the night before, so there was no sense in denying it or shying away from it. One thing she was learning real fast — with Werewolves, you had to stand your ground.

"No." Desmon shook his head. "There's no rule against wolves sleeping with humans. There is, however, a rule against other things involving consent and a full understanding of the commitment both parties are agreeing to, and that seems to be the rule that slipped Jason's mind in the heat of passion."

"What's the issue?" Brandi asked him. "It was an accident that I went into heat. We dealt with it. Why does it have anything to do with you?"

Jason snorted, the first smile of the day showing on his face. "She does have a point."

Desmon took another long drink of his coffee before he looked to Brandi. "You really think your accidental heat is the big issue here?"

"Isn't it?"

He just shook his head, looking exasperated for a long moment before he glanced back to Jason. "You better lay on that charm, because I don't want to deal with a fallout when she freaks and takes off. We have enough problems."

Jason sighed and looked at the table. "I've got it, Des. I told you I'd take care of it."

"Usually I'd believe that, but your track record isn't all that great this week."

"She's not unhappy here while we look for her attackers." Jason gestured to Brandi. "Are you?"

She shook her head. "No, but I'd like to call my friends and let them know I'm okay before they file a missing person's report for me."

Desmon seemed to agree with that. "What are you going to tell them?"

Brandi glanced to Jason, who seemed to be trying to silently communicate with her — and oddly enough, she understood what he was saying with that deep scowl. He really needed her to sell the idea to Desmon that their pack was safe with her. So she said, "I'll tell them my car broke down at a gas station. I mean, I don't actually have my car. They abandoned it in the woods so the cops wouldn't find it, but I guess I can deal with that problem later. I'll just tell her Jason helped me. We got rained in and he wasn't the worst company to get trapped with for the night."

Desmon tilted his head back and forth like he was considering it, and then pointed to Jason. "Let her make the call."

"Right now?" Brandi gaped at him. "In front of you?"

"I have a pack to protect, women and pups who are very vulnerable to the viciousness of the outside world. Can you imagine what your government would do if they found out about us? As much as I empathize with your situation, we don't typically broadcast to humans what we are. I'm not saying there aren't humans in our inner circle, but we're selective. I usually get to approve new members of our pack."

"I'm not the only wolf guilty of this," Jason cut in with a low growl. "It happens all the time. Wolves mate outside pack lines more than they do inside, and they're not calling you asking for permission before they do it."

"No, you're just the only one who did it with a human who has no knowledge of what she's gotten herself into."

Desmon's voice got lower, a little more growly, sounding slightly inhuman. "How do you know she won't expose us when she freaks out?"

"I wouldn't hurt children," Brandi said in insult. "You said you have young Werewolves you protect. I wouldn't put them in jeopardy, and if I haven't freaked out yet, I'm probably not going to. Trust me, I have had a lot of reasons to freak out over the past twenty-four hours. I'm still relatively sane. Is sex one time such a big deal?"

Desmon studied her for a long time, as if gauging her honesty, and then shrugged as though it was out of his hands. Then he glanced back at Jason, giving him a side-eyed look that made it obvious they were silently communicating. "You might want to give her your landline phone to make the call. The storm is messing up cell service. I haven't been able to reach Jazz. Of course, he's probably still out scouting with the others."

"That sucks." Jason got up from the table. "Last thing I need is company."

"It does suck for you. Big time. Unless this storm lets up, you're guaranteed company. That's what you get for living all by yourself out here on the north border. It's the only place they'll have to crash if they get sick of the rain. Jazz doesn't exactly have the same tact that I do, and he's the best of that crew. So I'd handle your situation as quick as possible."

Brandi got the impression Jason wasn't telling her something, but she didn't feel like hashing it out in front of this intimidating, if not extremely well-dressed alpha werewolf. So she made the call on the portable landline, feeling very self-conscious with both Jason and Desmon watching her like hawks…or wolves.

"Hello," Jenny answered on the first ring, sounding frantic.

Brandi felt guilty. "It's me."

"Oh my God!" Jenny took a shuddering breath. "We've been talking to the police. We thought you were dead in a ditch somewhere!"

"Jesus." Brandi put her head in her hand, feeling more guilt-ridden by the second, even though she almost *was* dead in a ditch. "I'm sorry. Are you okay? Did the stress affect the baby?"

"Me?" Jenny shouted in disbelief. "Where are you? What the hell is going on?"

"It's stupid. My car broke down. There's a horrible storm. We had no cell reception. I couldn't get through." Brandi winced at the series of half-lies, and then looked at the phone in her hand, wondering if the police could figure out it was a landline. "Jason's cabin got struck by lightning. It blew out everything. Even destroyed his home phone. We have no Internet either. I'm in a little town. Their cell service probably sucks on good days; with a storm like this, it's impossible. Jason's friend just brought over his landline so we could plug it in and make calls."

"Who the hell is Jason?"

"Um." Brandi looked to Jason, who was staring at her across the table. "He's, uh…" She hesitated, knowing Jenny probably wouldn't believe Brandi hooked up with a stranger, even though that's what actually happened. "I met him a few months ago. I was going to bring him with me as a surprise, but then my car broke down. We happened to be close to his hometown. He called his friends to pick us up, but when we got here, the skies opened up and I couldn't call. I am so, so, so sorry."

"You met a man and didn't tell me?" Jenny sounded thoroughly insulted. "Are you serious right now?"

"Surprise," Brandi whispered weakly.

She winced at Jason, realizing it may sound to him like she'd just turned their one-night stand into a months'-long relationship.

"I am so pissed off at you right now." Jenny broke into Brandi's thoughts with her annoyance. "I didn't sleep at all last night and now you're telling me I missed out on months of juicy gossip? What the hell? Is he hot?"

"Yes." Brandi didn't even hesitate.

"How hot? Like smoking hot?"

Brandi's cheeks flamed, but she didn't dare lie in case Jenny did meet Jason one day. "*Smoking hot.*"

"Chippendale-dancer hot? *Playgirl*-centerfold hot?"

Brandi's felt as if her whole face was burning up, but she had to say, "Hotter."

"Holy shit. I want a picture. Send me a picture right now," Jenny demanded, clearly forgetting the fear of Brandi being missing in action. "Do you know how worried I've been about you since the divorce? Send me a picture of you two together. I'll post it on Facebook. You know someone will show it to Carl. I'm still friends with his sister. Oh, please, please, please."

"No cell service," Brandi reminded her. "And I sorta lost my phone. I can give you Jason's number." She gestured to Jason, and he jumped up, getting the message. "That way you'll have it if you need to get in touch with me."

"Yeah, good idea. I actually called the police. I didn't have any proof that something terrible happened to you, so we had to wait to file a report, but we were walking out the door to get it done. I cannot believe you didn't tell me you had a Chippendale boyfriend!"

"What's a Chippendale?" Jason whispered to Desmon as he handed Brandi a paper he'd written his number on.

Desmon just shook his head and said under his breath, "Don't ask."

"Who is that?" Jenny asked. "Is that him? Is he there?"

"Yeah." Brandi looked at the paper with his number on it. "You ready for his number?"

"I want a picture, because something's off. I smell bullshit. You've been a total social recluse since the divorce. You're home every night."

Brandi covered her face, still completely mortified because she knew Werewolf hearing allowed both men to hear everything. Not to mention, signing Jason up for a fake relationship he probably didn't want to be in was the last message she wanted to send to him the morning after.

"Let's see, maybe we can get reception to send a picture." Jason wrapped an arm around Brandi, catching her off guard when she was still hiding her face.

"What?" she looked up just as he snapped a picture of the two of them together with his cell phone. "I have no makeup! I probably look like shit."

"No, you look beautiful," Jason assured her with a smile. "You always look beautiful."

"His voice is sexy," Jenny whispered, now completely distracted from Brandi dropping off the face of the earth. "Carl never said sweet things like that to you."

"Carl's an asshole," Jason half-growled it, sounding almost inhuman.

"Is he on the line?"

"No, he just has really good hearing," Brandi said with a glare at Jason.

She was starting to suspect Jason didn't spend much time with humans.

Desmon was glaring at him too.

Jason just shrugged. "Her ex *is* an asshole."

"Did he get service? Can he send me the picture?" Jenny went on, now sounding way too excited. "I'm practically your sister. It's not weird to need proof you're not being held captive by a psycho."

"My word should be your proof."

Jenny wasn't fazed. "I need more."

Brandi wrote Jenny's number on the same paper Jason wrote his on and waited for Jason to text the picture.

Jenny put her on speaker when she got the text, and then screeched in her ear. "You bitch! I cannot believe you are having a torrid love affair with that tall, sexy, buff-as-hell piece of —"

"Really good hearing," Brandi reminded her. "I have to go, Jen."

"I bet you do," Jenny said in a singsong voice. "So when are you two getting out here? When do I get to meet him?"

"My car." Brandi sighed because she had no idea if she'd ever see it again. "It's in bad shape."

"God, that car is brand new," Jenny said in disbelief.

"Soon," Jason said as he leaned in and spoke against the phone. "Brandi's told me all about you. We'll find a way to get out there. If we can't make it in her car, we'll take mine."

"I can't wait!" Jenny spoke louder than normal, obviously trying to make sure Jason heard her. "Take good care of her. Protect her from the big mean storm." Brandi got the impression Jenny was doing air quotes when she said "storm," because the sarcasm was dripping in her voice as she added, "Make sure you *stay warm*."

"Okay," Brandi said drily. "I love you. Call Jason's phone if you need anything."

"Sure thing," Jenny went on, still sounding very amused. "Don't get too wet."

"I have to go, Jen."

Brandi hung up the phone and set it down. She was certain her face was a violent shade of red as she dropped her forehead to her folded arms on the table and hid.

"I am so sorry," she mumbled against her arms. "I swear, I'm not going to turn into some crazy, clingy bitch who'll boil your bunnies after what happened last night. I just couldn't think of anything else."

"What are you talking about?" Jason sounded mystified.

"It's a movie reference." Desmon chuckled. "Besides, Jason doesn't boil bunnies. He roasts them, unless he's out scouting. Then it's rabbit tartar."

"Oh gross." Brandi lifted her head and turned to Jason. "Is that true? You eat bunnies?"

Jason met her look of disbelief with one of his own. "I'm a wolf. I eat pretty much anything I can catch."

"You can catch me," she reminded him, unable to help the shudder that came from the memory of yesterday. "Do a lot of Werewolves eat humans? Is that a thing with you guys?"

"Brandi, no," Desmon answered for him. "We like humans. Most Werewolves do. We're cautious for survival purposes, but we don't attack humans for no reason. Just like you have nuts in the human world who commit terrible, senseless crimes, we have them too, but we're going to take care of the ones who went after you. I promise. Our criminal justice system is much more swift and effective."

Brandi nodded, because something about Desmon was easy to believe.

"You're Jason's now. That means you're under my protection." Desmon reached across the table and squeezed her arm. "No one fucks with my pack."

"What do you mean I'm Jason's now?" Brandi asked.

"I thought I was your man." Jason's voice was low and husky as he leaned in and pressed a kiss against the curve of her neck. "Isn't that what you told your friend?"

"I'm out." Desmon stood up, but smirked at Jason. "Well played."

"It was a cover." Brandi's cheeks were hot again.

"I don't mind being your man for the time being." Jason kissed her again and then whispered against her ear. "Are you going to tell me what a Chippendale is?"

"No." Brandi shook her head, though she went back to hiding in the cover of her arms. "Don't you use your Internet?"

"Rarely." Jason sounded bored at the mention of it. "I'm an enforcer. I work outdoors. I'm not managing finances or buying real estate. What do I need to use the Internet for?"

Brandi turned her head on her arm. "Do you have a computer?"

"No." Jason shook his head. "I have my phone. That's all I need. We text with each other when we're scouting in skin. Desmon made sure we all know how to keep in touch."

"In skin?" she repeated.

"Instead of fur." Desmon raised his eyebrows at her. "They don't take their phones with them when they're shifted. Where would they put them?"

"Right, good point." Brandi dropped her head back to arms. "I need some of that coffee you guys are drinking without me."

"Take off, Des." Jason sounded amused. "I got this."

"I hope so." Desmon walked to the door, but the click of his expensive shoes against hardwood stopped. "I like her, Jason."

"Yeah, I like her too." Jason sounded so proud, Brandi had to lift her head and give him another curious look. He just gave her a devious smile and said, "It's not every day I find out I'm in a months'-long, semi-serious relationship with a sexy human."

"Coffee," Brandi decided as she hid her face in her arms once more. "Lots and lots of coffee."

Chapter Nine

Jason had planned on spending the day "laying on the charm," as Desmon called it. He needed to get to a place where he felt a little more comfortable before he explained to Brandi that he mated her for life and it couldn't be undone simply because he was rash about it.

Mates didn't do well being separated once they bonded.

It affected their mental and physical well-being. Jason didn't know many wolves who'd survived for long periods after they were separated from their mates. That's why bonding was treated with great reverence and caution, though sometimes it just happened like it did with Jason and Brandi. His mother had never been the same after his father left, but she'd had Jason, so that kept her going. Maternal instinct was a powerful motivator for survival, but she died way too young for a Werewolf, and he never once doubted it was his father's fault.

NIGHTWIND PACK: CLAIMED 151

It was unfortunate Brandi didn't understand anything about the natural laws that governed Werewolves. She'd essentially gotten married with no option of divorce, without knowing it. The mating also made her incredibly ripe to get pregnant, but Jason could smell Brandi was on birth control, which was why he hadn't bothered with condoms. Not like diseases were a concern…Werewolves had a lot of enemies, but disease wasn't one of them.

In the end, Jason did what he did best. More action, less words. He wanted to fix things for her, protect her, and make up for the pain she'd suffered at the hands of Werewolves. So he took a few wolves out and they tracked down her car, which was no easy feat when the storm had washed away all trace of it.

The assholes who'd tried to kill her must've moved it after the other wolves didn't turn back up. Jason finally found it clear over in Goodwin territory. Luckily, they got it without being detected by the rival wolves.

Brandi was so thrilled to get the car back, it made Jason want to spend the rest of his days playing hero for her.

He'd been concerned that she'd want to go home after she got her car, but he reminded her that they still needed to catch the wolves responsible for attacking her. He didn't trust them not to seek her out. It wasn't the only reason he wanted her to stay with him, but it wasn't a lie either. She agreed quickly, giving him the impression that hanging around a few extra days wasn't such a hardship, even if it was with a Werewolf.

Now it was night, and the storm still raged. There was horrible flooding in the valley. If it kept up, Jason was going to be spending his mating honeymoon rescuing wolves with houses in the lower sections of pack lands. He called Desmon to touch base and see if he needed help, but got no answer.

Which meant the phones were fucking up worse than he thought, or Desmon was dealing with larger issues and was too stressed out to be bothered with Jason.

So Jason left a message offering to help if it was needed.

They'd gone to the store and picked up food. Jason bought steaks, because it was already obvious he wasn't going to impress Brandi with his hunting skills.

Cooking with Brandi in the kitchen and having her there was nice. Comforting. Brandi suggested they watch television while they ate, except Jason didn't have a television. Then she grabbed one of her bags they'd brought in earlier from the trunk of her car, and pulled out her computer to put on something for them to watch.

She picked a modern spy film.

Brandi claimed it was the only man movie she owned.

Jason enjoyed it immensely, especially when Brandi curled up next to him on the couch after they were done eating. Their plates lay abandoned on the coffee table, and he should probably pick them up, but feeling Brandi against him was more appealing. She smelled amazing, and she felt so fucking good, all soft curves pressed against him. He kept turning away from the glare of the screen to glance down at her looking extraordinarily sexy in one of the nightshirts she got out of the bags she'd packed for the trip to visit her friend.

"He is effective, but he has no honor," Jason mused, as he watched the head spy callously dismiss the woman he was supposed to be protecting when she died. "He doesn't care she's dead. He makes a joke about it. Your men, they don't care at all for their women, do they? Like my father, they have no loyalty."

"Well, some do. There are good ones out there." Brandi lifted her head from where she was resting it against his chest to look up at him. "Or so I've heard."

"Our worlds are very different." Jason kept staring at the computer, watching as the spy left behind the dead woman without a backwards glance. "I would turn into a monster if someone killed you in front of me. Even the most terrifying stories humans created about our kind wouldn't touch what I'd be if someone did that."

She gave him a bemused smile. "That sounds oddly sweet, in a totally disturbing Werewolf sort of way. I didn't know you cared."

"I care," he promised her. "I'd protect you better than that guy could. I have skills he doesn't."

She laughed. "That's a tall order. He has some pretty impressive skills."

"So do I." He waggled his eyebrows. "In all ways, but I don't want his large collection of women." He pulled her tighter against him and squeezed her arm affectionately. "I only want this one."

Her smile became wide and pleased, making her cheeks flush, and Jason couldn't resist leaning down and kissing her. Brandi parted to him with a soft, feminine sigh that made his dick rock hard almost instantly. He slipped his tongue into her mouth, unable to taper his low growl of arousal, but Brandi didn't seem to mind. She kissed him back fiercely, in a way he never imagined a human could, until they were both breathless.

He'd pushed Brandi back against the couch and was partially draped over her when they finally parted for air. The movie was forgotten as Jason pulled up to study her. Her lips were red and swollen, and he rubbed his thumb over her bottom one. Brandi shuddered from that simple caress, making him realize the heat may have not totally been to blame for her raw, sexual responsiveness the night before.

It was just Brandi.

"Why'd you stay?" he asked, still breathing heavily as he fought to keep his carnal side at bay. "The real reason."

"So crazy Werewolves wouldn't attack and eat me." Her chest was heaving too, the deep V in her nightshirt showing off the curves of her full tits. "You said they could track me to my apartment."

"That's the only reason?" he pressed, because he needed to know if she felt it too, this inexplicable pull to be close, to fuck, to drown herself in this relationship even though they barely knew each other. He rubbed his thumb against her bottom lip again. She sucked in a sharp breath, and closed her eyes. Then she licked it, sending a rocket-fire pulse of lust straight to his dick. His hips jerked of their own accord, as he demanded, "Tell me."

His voice was rough with need.

"You're sounding very wolfy," Brandi teased.

"You're making me feel very wolfy." He let out a low, animalist growl that made her jerk back, but she was smiling, which meant she knew he wasn't a threat, so he pressed, "I want to know. Why'd you stay?"

"Because I didn't want to be eaten by crazy Werewolves." Her smile was back. "Not that this place is any better. I was practically molested when your friend just walked in and smelled something he liked."

"I said I was sorry about that." He dropped his head back to the curve of her neck. "Everyone in my pack knows I keep a spare key hidden on the porch. Paul let himself in probably thinking I was still out running with the pack." He kissed her neck, and she made one of those soft, purely feminine sounds that forced him to run a hand up her smooth, bare thigh. "Sometimes the men will show up here after a run and have some beers with me."

A howl sounded from outside, and it was close. Another one followed. Brandi jumped. Jason turned and eyed the locked door. He sighed, wondering if he was cursed somehow.

Unbelievable.

"Like tonight." He winced when she looked up at him with wide eyes. "Some of them are outside."

"Are you serious?" She sounded stunned. "It's raining like crazy. Why are they even out in this?"

"I can hear them talking. Jazz and a few of our other enforcers were still scouting for the wolves who tried to kill you. We take attacks on our land very seriously. Rain doesn't stop us."

"Jazz, the other alpha wolf?" She sounded even more panicked. "Is he going to come in here with a suit, barking orders and listening while I make phone calls too?"

"Not likely."

Jason winced again as he got to his feet, his body mourning the loss of Brandi. He still had a raging hard-on and the room reeked of desire. Something he was sure Jazz and his crew would notice, if they didn't smell that he was mated first.

Jason walked for the door, adjusting his dick in his jeans as he went. He pulled his shirt lower and then turned the lock. He could hear Jazz looking for the key under the mat. It was a sure bet they'd all walk right in. He blocked the door when he opened it, because there were four very naked Werewolves standing on the other side.

"Hey." He stared at Jazz with wide eyes, trying to silently communicate his situation. "Tonight isn't a good night."

"Don't want to lose your money, huh?" Jazz laughed as he shook his head in a very wolf-like manor, spraying Jason with water as he tried to dry his soaking-wet hair. "Move, Jason. This storm is killing us. We've been out there, in fur, in the pouring fucking rain for over twenty-four hours. I'm done. I need a beer and whatever leftover meat you caught for dinner."

Jazz sniffed the air. The rain and mud were obviously affecting his sense of smell, but he turned back to Jason with wide eyes. "The human is still here?" He leaned in, sniffing Jason, and then huffed in disbelief. "Did you—"

Jason gave him another look, hoping to shut him up. "I have company. It's *really* not a good time. Didn't Des ever contact you and the guys? I know he left you a message on your cell phone. You haven't been back to your place since yesterday?"

"Nope." Jazz let out a low laugh of disbelief. "But I bet he wants to kill you if he smelled what I am. How'd that even happen? You just met her. But let's discuss this inside. Like it or not, you're stuck with us for a while until this storm passes.

It's getting nasty out there. I don't want any of us caught in a mudslide."

"Why, are you afraid your human will find something she likes better if you let us in?" Luke taunted as he shook his head in the same way Jazz had.

Jason growled, and curled back his lip, showing off his fangs that had grown long. He was feeling more than a little territorial, and he made sure they all knew it.

"Really?" Jazz stared at Jason in disbelief. "He's kidding. We're not going to molest your human."

"Unless she wants us too," Caleb added.

Jason growled louder.

"Look, it smells to me like she's off the market. So why are you growling at us when we've been out scouting to protect her while you've been holed up in this cozy cabin with a sweet-smelling human?" Jazz gave him an unimpressed look. "Or maybe we interrupted something."

Even with the rain and the shock of Jason's scent changing now that he was mated, it was obvious Jazz could smell the desire still choking the air out of the room. He was fucking with Jason on purpose, likely since he'd been bored scouting in fur since yesterday.

Jason just sighed, knowing this could only get worse. He met Brandi's gaze as she looked at him over the edge of the couch. "You better close your eyes. Four naked men are about to walk in."

Brandi frantically shook her head no. "I don't have any pants on."

"Your shirt covers everything." Jason wasn't particularly thrilled about them seeing her in a nightshirt either, but it was long, hanging clear past her knees, and by Werewolf standards that was more than enough. "Close them or you'll see more of my friends than you probably want to, since you're such a stickler for clothing."

"So what, we're just going to stand here because your human has a thing about clothing?" Jazz asked in an unusual display of annoyance, which meant the days of rain and fur had worn on him. "Are we allowed to walk past her to take a shower?"

"I'll grab some clothes for everyone."

Jason dashed up the stairs, knowing the enforcers and Jazz were impatient and Brandi was anxious.

Bad combination.

Chapter Ten

Brandi watched Jason run up the stairs and then sat there on the couch, feeling exposed. Every hair on her body stood on end when she thought about the Werewolves behind her. She trusted Jason, but that was about it. Even Desmon had left her incredibly on edge in that dominant, scary-boss sort of way.

She was hyper-sensitive to what they were saying, even though they were talking in low voices by the door.

"All the rain and mud's messing up my smell. Like *mated* mated?" one of the Werewolves was asking.

"That's what I'm smelling." Jazz had a distinctive growly voice, lower than the others, more wolf-like in a way that sort of reminded her of Desmon. "And he didn't deny it."

"Jason hates humans."

Another wolf snorted. "But we haven't really seen what she looks like yet. There are exceptions to every rule."

"I can hear you," she decided to announce, before they said something *really* insulting.

"Hey, darlin', I'm sorry, but it *is* an honest question."

The way Jazz said it was reminiscent of Jason, how the word *darlin'* rolled off his tongue like a caress. She could tell without seeing him that Jazz the alpha was a man who was used to being obeyed. It made her feel vulnerable.

Then one of the men whistled.

And the others laughed.

Brandi squeezed her eyes shut tighter, but all she saw were those wolves hunting her in the woods.

"I'm Jazz." He sounded amused, almost playful. That was very different from Desmon. "You really don't have to be so shy. We're not human. Not like we have anything that needs hiding."

They all laughed again.

Even if he was more playful, less intense than Desmon, she could tell Jazz wasn't someone used to following rules. He didn't like being told to stand by the door.

Brandi heard the creak of the floorboards as he walked up to the couch, and she warned, "You're too close."

"We don't actually bite, you know."

"Unless you want us to," one of the other Werewolves offered.

That seemed to be his one good line.

Brandi wasn't impressed.

Behind her closed eyes, she was seeing those wolves in the woods chasing her, teeth gleaming and vicious. The threat of biting was very real to her. Brandi stopped closing her eyes and jumped off the couch instead. She headed towards the stairs while trying very hard not to look back at the Werewolves.

"Hey, hey, hey." Jazz caught her by lightly clutching Brandi's shoulder, clearly moving much faster than her. "We were just—"

Brandi reacted before he could finish. She grabbed his hand and used the maneuver her brother and his friends had taught her. She dipped her shoulder, and yanked with all her might.

It shouldn't have worked, but she did have an epic amount of adrenaline pumping through her veins. She heard gasps as the large man crashed on his back on the floor. Brandi saw the surfer-blond, extremely buff and naked Werewolf stare up at her with wide blue eyes filled with shock.

He rolled over, recovering instantly, and couched naked in front of her. He looked more wolf-like all of a sudden, tilting his head like he wasn't sure what to make of her.

He really *was* built. She could see the Nightwind tattoo on his thick, cut upper arm. He had wide shoulders and was muscular like Jason. Didn't they have any fat, out-of-shape Werewolves? Her gaze darted to the other three naked men by the front door. They were all muscular and in shape, with their matching Nightwind tattoos that was obviously a brand of some sort. Each of them were *Playgirl* material all the way.

She glanced back to the blond man still staring at her with shock.

"Shit," Jason cursed from above. "Don't touch her, Jazz. Please. Remember, she's human and she's got a mouth on her. What was that thump I heard?"

Jason ran down the stairs for Brandi.

One of the men by the door laughed. "She threw Jazz. Flipped his ass right over her body and onto the floor. I didn't know humans could do that. I thought that was a bitch-only move."

Jason jumped between Jazz and Brandi. Now all she had to stare at was Jason's naked back. She moved closer, until she was a breath away from him. Then she reached out and gripped his belt loop at the back of his jeans, needing the extra security.

Jason sighed and threw the clothes in his arms to the men. "Get dressed. She's offended by us naked."

Jazz, the blond, softly cursed. "What in the hell, Jason? You never dated a human in your life and you decided to mate with this one?"

Jason coughed loudly, and Brandi got the impression he was giving Jazz a look that silently communicated something. She was obviously right, because Jazz coughed too, only it sounded more shocked than anything.

"Are you shitting me right now?" Jazz barked in that low, growly wolf- like voice. "You didn't tell her? That's breaking at least three laws. Des is going to freak."

She wanted to ask. Brandi got the impression all day Jason wasn't telling her everything, but she wasn't going to press the issue in front of these strangers.

"He knows about it." Jason sounded a little miserable. "He told me to lay on the charm."

"Let me know how that works out." Jazz snorted. "And this is not one you want to piss off. She attacked me for no reason."

Jason turned his head and looked down at Brandi. "What happened?"

"He startled me."

"No one here would hurt you." He suddenly smiled. "You threw our second alpha, huh? That was brave. You touch most alphas and they'll kill you for something like that."

"He touched me first and instincts took over."

Jason frowned and looked back to Jazz, while the alpha wolf pulled on the sweatpants and a T-shirt.

"She was having a panic attack," Jazz explained. "I was trying to be nice and she had to go all ninja on my ass. I wasn't expecting it from a human. Now I'm the one who has to deal with never living that down."

Jason laughed.

Brandi smacked his back lightly. "Damn it, it's not funny. They were being flirty and talking about biting me like I was something tasty."

"It *is* funny." Jason turned his head, grinning, and looked down at her. "You just don't think so because it's happening to you. If you weren't so damn cute, the guys wouldn't keep hitting on you."

Brandi flipped him off.

Jason's grin spread. "Trouble, Brandi. Pure trouble. Behave and come out from behind me. Don't worry. I'll stay close. You do look tasty, but I'll keep the big bad wolves away."

She released his belt loop and eased to the side of him. The four men were dressed. The blond eyed her grimly.

She backed into Jason again, and he assured her, "They aren't going to hurt you. I was teasing. The only one who gets to bite you is me." She glared up at him, but Jason didn't seem fazed. "If you're going to be glued to my side, at least help me grab a few beers. They've been scouting in fur since yesterday. You do not want to know what they're surviving off of when they do that."

She didn't want to get close to the men, but helping Jason in the kitchen and gathering the beers to hand out at least kept her busy. Afterwards, Jason sat down at the table and pulled out the chair next to him. Brandi sat. She eyed the other four men at the table with her and Jason.

Jazz frowned at Brandi again and looked at Jason. "So what does Des want to do about this? She knows about us. If you fail at your charm plan—"

"She's no threat to us, Jazz." Jason's good mood seemed to wane. "I'll personally vouch for her, regardless of what happens. She took it like a champ. Hell, she's handling it damn well right now, don't you think?"

Jazz studied her once more, and then nodded. "She's your responsibility. Not that you don't already know that."

"You know I don't mind that responsibility. I'm happy to have it," Jason said, sounding almost insulted. "It's an honor, not a problem."

Something about the way he said it made Brandi feel sort of warm inside, safe in a way she hadn't in a long time, even if she *was* sitting at a big kitchen table with a bunch of strange Werewolves.

Then Jason laughed. "Sorry she flipped you on my floor."

Jazz grinned. "She surprised me. I wasn't expecting it."

One of the four men laughed. "A human tossed Jazz. I can't wait to tell everyone."

Jazz turned and scowled at him. "What?"

His friend's laugh died. "I won't tell a soul."

Jazz suddenly chuckled. "It's fine, Jim. I was teasing. It was funny."

Brandi opened her mouth. She wanted to tell them they were nuts. Jason caressed her thigh, and she looked to him.

"Behave. Whatever you were going to say, don't unless it's polite."

She shut her mouth.

Jason grinned and winked at Jazz. "She's feisty as hell."

"Never a bad thing." Jazz winced. "We need to stay here during the storm."

"I know." Jason nodded. "It's not a problem."

The front door banged open. Jason turned his head and inhaled, and then he sighed. "Full house tonight."

"Desmon must have had other teams scouting for mudslides. I bet they're taking shifts and they decided your place is the best resting point. Get out the sleeping bags, and if she doesn't like to see naked men, you better bring down a pile of clothes or take her upstairs and keep her there."

Jason reached over and put his hand over Brandi's eyes. "Five more just came in, so close your eyes or you're going to see more naked men. I'm going to go get more clothes."

Brandi shut her eyes, tense and nervous all over again.

Jason hesitated before leaving. "You're safe, Brandi."

"You keep telling me that, and then I have to hit someone or flip them."

Jason chuckled. "Right. Jazz, make sure no one touches her please. The knives are in here. I'd hate to get more blood on my floor tonight from her causing damage."

****

Brandi was a little drunk. She had stopped playing quarters with the Werewolves after a few rounds. They were ganging up on her and she knew she'd be passed out cold by now if she hadn't refused to play after they made her drink the equivalent of three beers. Jason stayed by her side so she felt safe.

The power had gone out, so they had to rely on candles and the fireplace for light. The storm outside was brutal. Eleven men total of Jason's pack had shown up to spend the night inside and avoid the sheets of rain coming down. The wind battered the cabin. They were in the living room, sitting around the coffee table, and she watched the men going through all of Jason's booze. The beer had gone first, then some bottles of wine he'd had stashed, and finally the hard stuff from his bar was on the table.

One of the men on the other side of Brandi suddenly reached over and brushed a finger down her arm. She jerked away from his touch.

Jason growled at the other man. "Don't touch her."

The man growled back.

Jason leaned over Brandi and grabbed the man's borrowed T-shirt. "I said, *don't touch her.* Stop drinking if you think you can take me because you're being stupid."

Jazz growled at both of them. "She's off-limits, Ted." He turned his gaze to Jason. "Maybe you should take her upstairs to your room. Some of us have drunk more than our share. She's tempting."

Jason nodded and released Ted. He stood up. "Come on, darlin'. Bedtime."

Brandi let Jason haul her up by her hands. She was a little unsteady on her feet. He grinned down at her. "Lightweight."

She smiled and took his hand when he offered it. He led her to the stairs. It was dark upstairs, but Jason seemed to see fine as he led her to his bedroom. Inside the door, he paused.

"Stand still. Let me turn down the bed."

She released his hand. "Okay."

Jason stepped away and she heard him moving in the room. She shivered. It was colder upstairs away from the fire. She wondered how chilly it would get in the winter upstairs. A hand touched her arm and she jumped.

Jason chuckled. "Relax. I shut the door. I even locked it. We're the only ones in here. I can see, and trust me, it's just us."

She smiled. "Okay."

Jason chuckled and tugged on her arm. "Do you have a preference on what side of the bed, because I'd prefer to sleep near the door so I can get up faster. We didn't really discuss it last time. Just kind of passed out."

She shrugged, feeling that nervous sort of tingle that rushed over her. It was so strong she wondered if she was still in heat. "Any side is fine with me."

"I have to light my heater, but I haven't done it. It's too early in the year even though it doesn't feel like it tonight. This storm wasn't supposed to be this bad. You'll have to rely on me to keep you warm."

Brandi laughed, but still her neck felt hot and her stomach jolted with anticipation. She'd never wanted a man like she did Jason. It was almost unnatural, her draw to him, but they had a house full of Werewolves.

They weren't doing *that* with all of them downstairs.

"The bed is in front of you." Jason guided her with his hand on her lower back. "Get in and be careful. Don't crawl over too far and fall. I'll take this side."

She climbed up on the bed. "I wish I could see."

He chuckled. "I can, and I like what I'm looking at."

She flushed and climbed to the other side, enjoying Jason's big, comfortable bed. She felt the mattress dip when Jason crawled into bed with her a good minute later. He tugged up covers, and then turned to face her as his arm went over her. He tucked her in, before he stretched out next to her and his bare leg brushed hers.

"You're naked," she accused him, and jerked her leg back because just feeling his skin against hers made her wet. Laughter came from downstairs. Brandi shut her eyes and whispered, "What are you doing? Aren't you tired?"

"I always sleep in the buff," he confessed, and she could almost hear the smile in his voice. "And you're in my bed, darlin'. You know I'm not tired. I may never sleep again. You're too much of a sexy distraction. How about a kiss goodnight for old times' sake?"

Brandi turned her head. With the electricity still out, it made their hideaway in the woods pitch black. All she could do was feel. "What?"

He chuckled. "You heard me. Kiss me goodnight."

"I know what Werewolf hearing is like. I'm not doing that with them downstairs."

"The storm is too loud for them to hear. Kiss me. Just once. I promise I'll behave."

"I doubt you'll behave. You're very naked."

"You're not. Unfortunately." He ran a hand over her thigh, and then slipped it beneath the shirt to grasp her hip "Face me."

She slowly turned. "I can't see a damn thing."

"Close your eyes and relax. One kiss. I don't bite." His hand brushed her cheek. "At least not hard."

"That's a joke, right? Because I have proof you *do* bite hard."

Jason chuckled.

"Jason?"

"Relax." He was closer and she felt his breath on her face.

She shut her eyes and tried to relax. His mouth brushed hers gently. His touch was feather-light across her lips with his.

"See? That was innocent enough."

She arched her eyebrows. "That's your idea of a kiss? Ja—"

He captured her lips once more before she could finish and there was nothing gentle about this one. She gasped from the adrenaline shot of lust as his tongue explored her mouth. He slid his fingers into her hair, and then wrapped them around her nape. He shifted on the bed, moving closer as his mouth claimed hers.

The man could kiss. No wonder she kept getting into trouble where he was concerned. It was the only reasonable thought that entered her mind as she reached out and flattened her palms against his hard chest. His skin was firm and hot. She couldn't resist touching him, caressing him. Jason growled softly into her mouth, but like the night before, it didn't scare her. Not anymore. It turned her on. There was something wild about Jason that had her always wanting to get closer.

She pressed herself against him to feel the brush of his hard cock against her hip and moaned into his mouth. He let go of her nape to teasingly run his hand over her shoulder and down to her wrist. Then he let his arm slide under the covers, and was touching her thigh once more. Jason pushed up the shirt she was wearing so he was rubbing her hip. He grabbed her ass with one large hand, squeezed, and pulled her closer to his body.

Brandi felt his large erection trapped against her lower stomach. She lifted her leg and wrapped it around Jason's thigh on instinct, needing to be closer. She was still touching his thick, muscular chest before she slid one hand lower between their bodies.

Jason's mouth tore away from hers. They were both breathing hard. "Let me," he rasped into the inky darkness.

She opened her eyes, wishing she could see his face. "Let you what?"

When he moved away from her, Brandi wanted to protest. The comforter and sheet were torn from her body. Still blind as a bat, she jumped when he grabbed both her legs. She tensed for a second as Jason brushed his hands over the tops of her thighs and went higher. He gripped the boxer briefs she'd slipped on earlier over her panties when the house filled with Werewolves. He tugged them down, taking her panties with them.

"Lift your ass," he said softly. "I want to taste you again."

She shivered from memories of the first time, and lifted her hips. Jason tossed aside her clothes, and then gripped her knees. He was always so unbelievably strong, and he maneuvered her body easily. He pushed her knees up almost to her chest, spreading her thighs wide.

"You're so damn sexy," he whispered. "Stay just like that. Grip your knees for me."

Brandi only hesitated a second or two, then she did as he asked, figuring embarrassment had died the night before. She jumped when Jason's hot mouth brushed the inside of her thigh. She shut her eyes and took a shaky breath as the tease of it made her tingle.

"That's it, darlin'. Stay open for me and keep real quiet, okay? Can you do that?"

She nodded her head, knowing he could still see her in the darkness. "Okay."

He chuckled and his mouth brushed her other thigh. His hands left her before she felt him spread her wide open with his thumbs. She tensed a little, and then relaxed. She wanted Jason one more time. She wanted him to touch her again. He was unlike any man she'd ever met—in so many ways. He turned into a wolf. That should terrify her, but when it was

Jason, it was somehow okay. A sigh escaped her lips, and then a moan followed as Jason swiped his tongue over the full length of her pussy.

"So good," he growled softly. And reminded her, "Keep nice and quiet for me."

He came back at her fiercely. His mouth was hot and dominating as he licked her. His lips closed over her. He entered her with his tongue, pushing inside. The sudden and unexpected entry made her moan and throw her head back. Then he licked upwards, finding her clit. He used his strong tongue there, holding her open with his thumbs for maximum sensation.

Brandi thrashed her head and bit her lip to keep from crying out as Jason teased and tormented her. His teeth brushed her and she whimpered from the overwhelming pleasure. It didn't hurt. It felt incredible.

His mouth suddenly closed over her clit again and he sucked, using his tongue to flick her fast and strong.

Brandi gritted her teeth. Her stomach clenched. She couldn't take it. Her body bowed and she released her knees. She slapped her hand over her mouth and cried out into her hand as she climaxed hard. The bliss tore through her as her body jerked violently and her legs wanted to clamp together.

She couldn't close them though because Jason had suddenly gripped the insides of her thighs, holding them wide open as she climaxed. He forced her to stay completely exposed to him and she loved it more than she wanted to admit.

He tore his mouth away from her and growled softly, making him seem every bit the predator. In seconds he climbed over her, using his hips to force her thighs wider, and pinned her under him with his broad, muscular body. He grabbed her hand that was still locked over her mouth and yanked it away before he captured her lips with his.

She moaned loudly into his mouth as he entered her. He was so thick it made every nerve ending inside her come alive with ecstasy. Steel-hard, he slowly pushed in while spasms still gripped Brandi from her first orgasm.

She clutched at his shoulders, her nails digging in because Jason felt so large in her as he pushed deeper and deeper, until it was hard to know where she ended and he began. He groaned into her mouth and held still, locked deep and tight in Brandi as her muscles clenched and unclenched.

He was shaking too, making it obvious he was overwhelmed with her. Then Jason withdrew and drove back into her. The sensation made her gasp against his lips. She tried to tear her mouth from his, but Jason's hands were suddenly tight in her hair, holding her head immobile as he claimed her mouth with his tongue. He swallowed every moan as he moved on her, in her, riding Brandi fast and hard. She wasn't sure she could survive; it felt so good that it almost hurt.

All she could do was lock her legs around his driving hips and hold on. She could feel every hard inch of him as he pounded into her. Then her body tensed again and she screamed into his mouth as she climaxed once more. Pleasure ripped through her as Jason went taut over her. He growled and she felt his chest vibrate with the low, primitive sound. His hips jerked against hers in tight thrusts. Then she could feel the warmth of his cum as he started swelling inside her, dragging out the gratification of her orgasm for what felt like forever just as he had the night before.

Jason used his arms to keep his upper body weight from crushing her. His mouth left hers. They were both panting. Little pulses of pleasure continued to ricochet through her body, and Brandi realized her nails were still digging into his back. She released him but kept her eyes shut. She wasn't sure she had the strength or the will to open them anyway. Jason kissed her neck and turned his head, nuzzling her face with his.

"Damn, darlin'," he rasped. "I will never get sick of that."

She stayed wrapped around his large, powerful body, both of them sweaty and sticky as they lay there skin against skin. Brandi wasn't cold anymore, instead she felt warm, cozy and content. She smiled, thinking Jason had turned her into melted goo under him.

Jason brushed another kiss on her neck. "You okay?"

"Way better than okay."

He chuckled. "I think my nuts turned inside out."

Brandi grinned. "Inside out, huh? Is that a compliment?"

"I never came so damn hard in my life. It only feels like this with you, and that's not bullshit."

"I know. Me either. Something about you makes it really good. Straight sex never did it for me before this happened between us."

"Straight sex? You sleep with girls?" Jason sounded shocked.

Brandi ran her fingers over his sweaty shoulders. "No. I meant—"

Jason laughed. "I know. I was messing with you. Now I think I can sleep. How about you? Not minding me sleeping in the buff now?"

She grinned. "I'd never complain about that. I just didn't love the idea of your crew downstairs listening to us."

"I'm marking my calendar. That's a special event for you not to complain."

She swatted his back. "Don't be a jerk. Not after this."

He chuckled. "I could collapse on you and sleep right here inside you."

"You'd crush me."

Jason lifted his head and brushed his mouth against hers. She returned the kiss, before he pulled back and said, "I wouldn't want to crush you. You're a little thing. I'm rolling us, but I'm not leaving your body. I'm exactly where I want to be."

She was shocked when he rolled them all the way over, still buried deep inside her, so she ended up lying on him. He ran his hands down her back to her ass before he grabbed it possessively. "I love your soft little ass."

Brandi turned her head and got comfortable on Jason. She could hear his heartbeat under her ear as she smiled and drifted to sleep.

Chapter Eleven

The bedroom door came crashing open. Jason reacted faster than Brandi could. He rolled, his body withdrawing from hers as the comforter was thrown over her.

The bedroom was awash in early morning sunlight. Confused and still fighting off deep sleep, Brandi stared at the man framed in the bedroom door. Then her gaze jerked to a naked Jason who was standing next to the bed, putting himself between her and the attacker.

"Get out!" Jason growled.

The man was someone Brandi had never seen before. He wasn't one of the men from last night. He was about thirty, with blond hair. Like all Werewolves she'd met, he was thick and muscled. He growled at Jason, making it obvious he was definitely one of them as he moved into the room. Brandi grabbed the comforter and yanked it up to her chin when she saw him staring at her. The Werewolf looked furious, and was terrifying because of it.

"I said get out," Jason snarled.

The man sniffed the room. He growled back at Jason. "Where is she?"

The low rumble of fury that came from the center of Jason's chest was completely inhuman. "Not here, Kurt. Get the hell out of my room, and while you're at it, get the hell out of my home! I didn't invite you here."

"Where the fuck is my mate?"

Jason reached down and grabbed his jeans from the floor. He snarled curses as he jerked them on. "Why in the hell do you think your mate would be here? I wouldn't touch her if you paid me, and you have a lot of fucking nerve breaking in my bedroom door looking for her."

Brandi heard pounding, and then four more men were in the bedroom. Jazz and three of the men from last night showed up. Jazz only wore sweatpants. His broad, muscular chest was bare. His blond surfer hair stood up at odd angles, but his easygoing demeanor was gone as he snarled, "What in the hell is going on?"

"Kurt thought he'd break in my fucking door looking for his mate. She's not here. She's *never* been here. You know I wouldn't touch her." Jason sounded violent as he turned back to the intruder. "What is your problem? Do you have a death wish? Do you want to challenge me? You stormed into my home and broke down my bedroom door."

"I smelled female and sex. Noreen is good at masking her scent, so she smells different, even to me. She's made it a hobby of hers, and I know damn well she's after you," Kurt accused Jason with a snarl. "She talks about you and tells me how much she wants you."

Jazz cursed. "Your mate is not right, Kurt. We've told you to get her under control or you need to find a new home. This is the kind of shit we're talking about. We had to crash here last night because of the storm and I'll personally guarantee that your mate was never here."

Kurt took a deep breath. "I can't find her, Jazz."

Jazz groaned, some of the tension leaving his broad shoulders. "We can send a few people to the last location she was at to see if they can track her, but you need to get a handle on her. You can't go around making wild accusations and breaking in wolves' doors at seven in the morning."

"It's not my fault. She hasn't been right since her accident."

"This is not our problem! We have our own issues." Jason turned and eyed Brandi. He growled as he turned back to Jazz. "And where the hell were you four when he was breaking in? I have three enforcers and an alpha in my home and no one heard him?"

"We were sleeping. Like you." Jazz pointed down the hallway unapologetically, reminding them of the guest bedroom he crashed in. "I guess the guys downstairs are still too drunk and tired from fighting the flood."

"Just get out. I want everyone to get the hell out! This many males looking at her is making me irrational! I'm about to kill someone just because I fucking feel like it and you're at the top of the list, Kurt!"

Kurt obviously wasn't too bright. He didn't seem to want to leave; instead he looked around Jason, as if expecting Brandi to morph into his mate.

"Out." Jazz shoved Kurt none too gently. "As you can see, the female in Jason's bed isn't your mate. She's Jason's mate. This is supposed to be his honeymoon, so unless you feel like dying, get the fuck out."

"What?" Brandi gasped.

Jason growled and jumped so fast all the men stumbled back. Except Jazz, who stood his ground without fear, but he did wince. "It just slipped out. I haven't had coffee yet."

"It's not raining anymore. I want them all out of my cabin." Jason pointed at the door. "Now!"

All the men disappeared quickly, and Jazz said, "You were putting it off too long anyway," as he closed the door behind him.

"What is he talking about?" Brandi asked, knowing the men walking down the hallway could probably hear her. "Why is he saying we're on a honeymoon? Is that some sort of Werewolf joke for one-night stands?"

Jason's dark eyes looked at her with an emotion she couldn't gauge. He took a deep breath. "I did something without asking you first and I shouldn't have, but the urge was unexpected and overwhelming."

She gaped at him, not liking the sound of that. "What did you do?"

Jason folded his arms over his broad chest. "Do you want the good news or the bad news first?"

"The good news," she started hesitantly. "I think."

"The first time we came together, I bit you pretty hard." Jason spoke slowly, like he was choosing his words carefully. "And I partially shifted when I did it. That's, um…a unique combination. Shifting and biting at the same time during sex, it's actually illegal in my world to do with a human without warning her of the consequences, which is why Des and Jazz were so pissed at me. They could smell I did it the second they got near us."

Brandi let his words sink in and she felt the blood leave her face. "I'm going to turn into a wolf now, aren't I?"

He shook his head. "I didn't finish it. Right now, you're just immune to disease. Your aging process has slowed and you'll heal much faster, but you're still human. I could turn you all the way if you wanted me to."

"No," she said instantly and looked away. "No, thank you."

Jason frowned. "Is it so bad to be like me? You don't know the freedom, darlin', of changing and running in the woods. Your vision is better, your sense of smell. Hell, it's like a whole new world opens up around you."

She turned to face him once more. "The fleas, the ticks, sprouting a tail without warning, the fact that you have an uncontrollable desire to fetch."

Jason's eyes widened before he laughed. "I don't have an uncontrollable urge to fetch and the fleas don't like our blood. Ticks either. And even if they did, when you change back to skin they wouldn't have fur to hide under anymore."

"I am what I am, Jason. I wouldn't ask *you* to change. Don't ask me."

He stared at her for a long minute, and then nodded. "I accept that. It's going to make our life a little more complicated, but we'll be fine."

"How is it going to complicate our lives?"

Jason's grin faded. "My world is different from yours."

"No shit. Really?"

He laughed again. "I love your mouth and the things you say. You make me smile all the time."

"Thanks. Now get to the bad news. You and your friends have been acting strange since yesterday. Strange for Werewolves, that is, and you're already strange by default."

Jason was quiet for a long time rather than laughing at her joke, and then he finally admitted, "I mated you that first night, Brandi. That's why it's illegal to do it without explaining it first. It bound us together, but it was an instinct, almost like breathing, and I don't regret it. I can't. From the moment I found you running for your life in the woods and I saw how you were still fighting to the end, I knew you were the woman for me."

She was shocked. "What does mated mean exactly?"

"It means we're…" Jason looked away for a second, and then he glanced back and locked his gaze with hers again. "It's like marriage in my world. I married you. It made you mine and it makes me yours too. We belong to each other. Forever."

She was speechless.

Jason shifted where he stood, looking anxious. "Speak to me. Say something."

Brandi just stared at him.

"I know I should have asked but damn it, you were in heat and I wasn't thinking clearly either." Jason sighed. "I promise you a great life. I'll always protect you and your happiness will always come before my own. We have a nice home. We have room for children. I know it's kind of remote out here, but it's really not. There are a lot of homes in the woods of other mated couples and their families. The majority of the unmated males live at the pack house in town. You'll make plenty of friends, and if you want to work, I won't try to stop you. I'd prefer you stay home, especially if you agree to have kids with me, but either way I'll support you. Our pack is human friendly now that Des and Jazz took over. Our children would be protected even if they can't shift. I just want you to be happy. That's all that matters. I'd even—" Jason swallowed hard, as if he was trying to say something especially difficult, "I'd move to your world if you don't like it here. I'd do that for you. I'd leave my pack for you, and I know you don't understand how hard that is for a wolf, but it's huge."

Brandi's mind was spinning. She'd gotten married and hadn't even known it. She just stared up at Jason. He'd stopped talking and was watching her with his beautiful eyes. He looked so worried.

He should be.

"Talk to me. Yell at me. Just say something."

"Something," she choked out.

Jason laughed. "You always make me laugh. Say something about what you're thinking or feeling."

"Shocked. Deeply shocked."

"I know. It happened fast."

"Fast?" She shook her head at him. "We met three days ago, had sex a few times, were almost killed a few times more than that, and now you're telling me we're married?"

"The sex is pretty fucking fantastic," he reminded her as he crawled onto the bed. He got under the covers and pulled Brandi to him. "And I love sleeping with you in my arms." He pressed a kiss against the curve of her neck. "I'm falling for you. Hard."

"I guess that's good since we're married."

He grinned. "You're taking this well. Jazz and Des thought you'd come unglued. Jazz even told me to hide the knives when I finally told you

"Jason, I don't even know what to say."

"Then don't. Kiss me."

Jason shifted her in his arms, because he was so unbelievably strong. He lifted her like she weighed nothing, and then turned Brandi so she was straddling his lap. He brushed strands of wild, curly hair off her forehead and cupped her face in his large hands.

"You're all I want, Brandi. I won't be like your ex-husband. Mates are for life. They don't cheat. You're the only woman I'll ever touch and I'll kill any man who touches you. Any other wolf you meet will know it because of your scent that's tied to mine. You're safe with me," he promised her. "Your happiness comes before my own. You are my world, and my loyalty is yours before any others, including my pack. I wasn't lying when I said I'd move to the human world with you if that's what you needed to be happy."

Her heart almost skipped a beat. Jason was telling her he belonged to her, that he'd never cheat on her and would stay loyal forever. Then she frowned, more than a little skeptical, because life had taught her if something seemed too good to be true, it probably was. "If that's true, what happened with your buddy Kurt and his mate?"

Jason sighed. "That's something that can happen with my kind. They didn't have a love match to begin with, and then his mate had an accident. Her mind isn't right anymore. She's kind of crazy."

"So if you don't fall in love with me you can cheat on me?"

Jason shook his head. "Their mating was arranged by their families and they both agreed to it. Hell, I don't even think they liked each other. We have a bonding. Don't tell me you feel nothing for me." He almost looked afraid for a split second, before his gaze grew hard, as if he was hiding on instinct.

"Jason." She reached down and cupped his face like he'd done to her. "You scare me because of how much I feel for you. It's happening too fast

"There's no such thing." He grinned, the tension slipping out of him as easily as it showed up. "We follow our animal instincts and they're usually right. Mine were yelling at me to claim you because I know in my heart you're my mate. My animal knows it, and so do I."

"I don't have an animal hiding out under my skin. I'm just plain ol' human and I'm scared to death."

He laughed. "Humans are animals too. You just don't grow fur and...what did you call it? Sprout a tail? And you don't follow your instincts like we do. We're free with both halves of ourselves. You could become like me. I could change you."

"I'm not ready for that yet."

He nodded. "We have time."

She stared at him. "Do we have a time limit?"

He shook his head. "I could change you now or in fifty years. If you want to stay the way you are, I'm happy with that as long as you're happy with it.

She lifted her head and brushed her lips over his. She smiled at him when he pulled back. "Next time you partially shift inside me, you better tell me because if I'd seen that, I would've freaked out."

He nodded. "I *am* sorry. When we mate, I need to sink my teeth into you and I need to do it in both forms. I have to keep my teeth locked in. It's something in our saliva. You're going to smell like me now. All of my kind will take one whiff of you and know you're mine and you're mated."

"Are you going to do that again? Change while we're having sex," she asked hesitantly. "Is this something I need to be on the lookout for?

"It was a one-time thing. I'd never do that to you unless you decide to change over and we're both wearing fur."

"That's so not funny."

"It's a little funny," he said with a laugh.

She was quiet for a while, before she whispered, "So we're married?"

"Not legally like in your world, but in mine, hell yeah." He grinned. "Want a honeymoon, darlin'? I know I want one. I want to spend a few days in bed with you."

"I haven't agreed to it, Jason."

His smile faded and he lightly growled at her. His eyes narrowed. "You're mine. I'm yours. I'm not letting you go. *I can't.* It would tear my heart out of my chest. Don't ask me to let you leave me. Anything but that."

She didn't see anger in his gaze. She saw raw pain and fear, and it was too much for her. She shut her eyes and kissed him instead. Jason rolled her over and shifted his hips until she was under him again. Then he reached down and pulled at the button to his jeans. "I guess I'll just have to work harder at convincing you if you're going to be stubborn about it."

She smiled. "I won't argue with that."

Chapter Twelve

"No," Jason snarled.

Jazz and Desmon sat shoulder to shoulder across the table from Jason and Brandi. The two of them were as different as two alpha wolves could be, but they'd been best friends since they were pups. They each had different strengths, and were able to compensate for the other's weaknesses. It made them almost invincible as a team, and more than a little intimidating.

Very few wolves were capable of standing up to them, but Jason added,

"Not just no, but fuck no!"

Jazz frowned, then he looked over to Desmon. "He seems really opposed to your plan."

Desmon ran his fingers through his long black hair, and his shoulders were noticeable tense, since he was wearing jeans and a T-shirt today. "I know she's your mate and you're protective of her, Jason, but we need to draw this asshole out. We've got patrols all over the place. We're stretched thin because of the flood cleanup. It's been days and there's been no sign of trouble. Someone brought your mate here to challenge us. I doubt they changed their mind. They are biding their time. We need to get the alpha out of hiding and deal with him. I give you my personal promise she'll be safe. Let her decide."

Jason growled, everything in him opposing their plan. He shook his head, but Brandi turned to Jason and shrugged, like risking her life wasn't worth more than the casual gesture.

"No," Jason said softly as he looked down at her. "I won't have you in danger."

"They could grab another woman like they did me." Her voice was soft, reasonable, as if begging him to understand. "What if one of your pack isn't out there like you were when you saved me? I know what it's like to be kidnapped from my life, terrorized, and chased like an animal, all the while knowing the horror of what they planned on doing to me. I lived it and was almost torn apart by those bastards. It's a good plan, and you said yourself that asshole will be looking for me since I saw his face."

"It's my job to protect you." Jason was furious, and he knew his voice betrayed the wolf in him. "You are asking me to go against my nature."

Brandi leaned into him and ran her fingers through his hair. Her touch calmed him — and she knew it because he told her so the night before. She rubbed his chest and even undid a few buttons on his shirt to touch his skin. He loved the skin-to-skin contact and she used it to her advantage, but he still looked away from her rather than give in.

"You *will* protect me." Brandi reached up and touched his face, forcing him to look back to her until their gazes locked. "You'll be there. I know I'm safe. You killed three wolves to save me. This time you'll even have help. We need to find this terrible alpha before he takes another woman. I can't live with knowing it's going to happen and do nothing about it." She gave him a desperate, pleading look. "Please, baby?"

Jazz chuckled. "Baby?"

Jason jerked his face out of her hold and growled at Jazz.

"Hey, Sorry." Jazz looked unfazed. "I just never thought I'd see the day someone would call you a baby and not get their asses beaten."

Brandi turned and shot Jazz a dirty look. "You're not helping, and for your info, I call him that because he loves my breasts."

"Oh. Got it." Jazz laughed. "Kinky for a human. I guess you got more wolf in you than we thought. Are you sure he hasn't changed you?" His gaze went to Brandi's breasts. "But, I see the draw. It would put me in a mindset to want to put my mouth—"

Jason snarled. "Don't look at her!"

Desmon was grinning. "Jazz, maybe you should go outside? You're aggravating him more."

"It's good for him. Like you, he's way too intense." Jazz snorted with amusement when Jason growled again. "I'll go."

He walked out of the cabin looking completely unremorseful.

"Think about it," Desmon said softly. "I'll go outside and let you two talk about this. It's between mates. I'll give you privacy to discuss it, but I need an answer."

Desmon followed his best friend and left the cabin.

Once they were alone, Jason shook his head. "It's too dangerous. I don't want you to be a target."

"I understand, but I want to help catch this bastard." Brandi sighed, looking so incredible earnest despite the scent of fear clinging to her. "He laughed when he told me to run for my life, like it was funny to him that he was sending four of his men to tear me apart and leave my body parts in the woods. I want to stop it from happening to someone else. I know you'll keep me safe. I trust you with my life, Jason, but I want to do this. I want you to support me on doing this."

Everything in him wanted to fight against it, but he growled in defeat. "I am not happy, but I'll support your decision, darlin'. I know why it's important to you, but I want to warn you that if you're there when I get my teeth into that bastard, it's going to be brutal and blood is going to rain down on your apartment. You might want to take an umbrella with you."

She smiled up at him. "I saw one by your door. I'll take it with me."

He slowly smiled. "I'll keep you safe."

"I know you will. There's no doubt in my mind."

"I wish you'd let me change you over first. You'd be stronger and faster."

She shook her head. "Even if I were willing, you heard Desmon. The fact that I'm still human is going to make him come after me. If you changed me, I'd be a wolf and he might not want me."

"You smell like wolf. You're my mate."

"And you heard Jazz. Perfume will confuse their noses long enough to let them think I'm just regular human, like I was when they caught me. We needed to go by my apartment anyway. I'm down to one bra. You broke the straps to the other one on purpose."

He laughed. "I was in a hurry to get you naked. Would I really destroy your bra on purpose?"

She stared up at him, a smile tugged at her lips, and she didn't even hesitate before she said, "In a heartbeat."

Jason laughed and held up his hands. "I'm guilty."

"Go tell them we'll do this. I want to get it over with."

Jason's smile died; the pain of agreeing made his chest hurt, but he did it anyway. "All right."

****

Brandi let Jason go and walked upstairs, desperate for a few minutes alone to clear her thoughts. She sat on their bed and took deep breaths to still the wild surge of panic that was making her heart beat rapidly out of control.

She was putting her life in danger to catch a killer. That terrible alpha who set her up to be murdered in the most brutal way possible needed to be caught. He'd masterminded her abduction for nothing more than territory, and he trained his pack to be mindless killers. She'd survived this much. Brandi knew she could do this, and she'd have Jason there to protect her.

Gathering her nerve, she stood and headed downstairs again. She found Jazz and Desmon standing in the living room next to Jason, and forced a smile. "So when do you want to do this?"

"Today." Desmon eyed her for a second before he admitted, "I sent one of my men to your apartment yesterday. He smelled wolf. That other pack's been watching your place."

A fresh surge of fear slammed into her when she thought about that alpha stalking her home, but she pushed it down as Jason walked over to her.

Brandi knew he could smell her fear, and gave him a smile. "I'm okay."

He wrapped his arms around her protectively. "It's not too late to change your mind, darlin'. I'm hoping you will. We'll catch them sooner or later."

"But later will mean after someone else dies," she said softly. "Let's just do this and catch the bastard."

Jason nodded grimly, and then leaned down to press a kiss against her forehead.

Desmon cleared his throat. "She needs to bathe in scented soap. I bought scented lotion too. I even obtained clothing worn by a human female from town. She's a friend to the pack. You know Roni from the bar in town, Jason. We told her what was going on and she agreed to lend us some of her clothing and her home. All of it will hide your scent on your mate. You're going to have to resist the urge you'll experience to get your scent back on her. I hear it's a strong impulse when a mate doesn't smell like you anymore."

Jason nodded. "I understand."

Desmon looked to Brandi. "We're going to drive you to Roni's house. You'll take your bath there and we'll stay back so there's no scent transfer from us. Roni is lending you her truck to drive, that way you'll smell like another human and not us. We're going to be following you in two cars. All you have to do is drive to your apartment and wait. We'll be outside to protect you. When shit hits the fan, you lock yourself inside somewhere safe. We already have one car at your place with two other enforcers there as back up."

She took another long, steadying breath. "Okay."

"Let's go." Desmon eyed Jason, before he said solemnly, "We'll protect your mate with our lives."

"I know that." Jason nodded. Then he turned and suddenly grabbed Brandi. He lifted her up in his arms and hugged her.

She wound her arms around his neck, clinging to him as tightly as he held her. "I'm going to be fine, baby."

Jazz laughed. "Sorry," he chuckled. "It's just that now every time I hear her call you that, I see you with a breast in your mouth. Mental image."

Jason growled and planted a kiss on Brandi's lips. He was completely unapologetic as he looked down between them, eyeing her tits as he said, "And what nice breasts they are."

Brandi laughed. "Can you put me down now?"

He shook his head. "Let's go."

Jason not only carried her out to Desmon's waiting SUV, but he made Brandi sit on his lap in the backseat, holding her tightly the entire ride. She let him do it without complaint. He was worried about her safety and she knew it. She was scared too, so she hugged him back.

Jazz turned in the front passenger seat and frowned. "She's going to be safe, Jason. Do you honestly think we'd let him hurt your mate?"

"She's human," Jason said softly. "One wound could kill her. She's so damn fragile. You have no idea how fragile she is."

"You think I have no idea?" Jazz sounded almost insulted. "You *know* I get it. You know Des does too. We'll protect her, Jason. They won't even get close enough to see the color of her eyes."

Jason hugged Brandi tighter rather than respond, and she almost winced. "Speaking of fragile, you're about to crush me."

Jason eased up on his hold and brushed a kiss against her forehead. "Sorry."

Brandi smiled at him. "Never be sorry for hug injuries."

"What about sex ones?" he asked playfully.

She laughed. "That depends on how good it feels when they occur and what you did to cause them."

Jason hugged her once more. "I know the circumstances sucked, but I'm almost grateful to those assholes for what they did to you. It brought you into my life."

She nodded. "I know."

Brandi studied Jason. In just days, this man had become everything to her. He was loving, protective, fun — and she loved him. Staring into his eyes as he held her tightly on his lap, she knew she loved him more than she'd ever loved anything in her life.

Jason rubbed her thigh and asked, "What's that look for? It looks like you want me, and I like it a hell of a lot."

She smiled. "Ask me tonight when we're alone."

"Sex fantasy?" Jason's grin grew wide and devious. "I love your fantasies."

"Well, I do have a few of those." She laughed. "I have a vivid imagination."

Jason softly growled at her. "Want to share?"

"Wait until later," Jazz groaned from the front seat. "The scent of you two makes me hard and it's just mean to torture your co-alpha. Your mate is getting more aroused, Jason, so knock it off."

"Ask me if I care if you're uncomfortable," Jason asked. "I'm still pissed we're doing this in the first place."

"She does smell distracting, and I assume you want us focused for this job," Desmon said from the driver's seat. "Let's get this over with, and then Jazz and I will stay on the other end of pack lands until the honeymoon is over. You can do all the kinky human sex things you want."

Brandi flushed and Jason winked at her. "Great noses, and you do smell *very* good when you get turned on."

She shifted on his lap, purposely rubbing against the hard ridge under her ass. Jason bit his lip and his eyes narrowed. Brandi grinned at him and moved again, rubbing him with her ass.

"Keep it up," Jason warned her. "And I'll ask Des to pull over right here in the woods. They can stay in the SUV while I take you out there and show you what you're doing to me."

She laughed, because she needed the teasing to break the fear and tension of what she was about to do. Jason grinned, making it obvious he needed the games more than Brandi did.

"No time." Desmon shook his head with a snort of amusement. "Sorry. We need to get to Roni's and I want to be at Brandi's place by dark. It's a long drive."

Jason groaned and asked Brandi, "How far away did you live?"

"Almost two and a half hours away."

"Shit." Jason eased her off his lap. "You better sit there, darlin', or I'll end up embarrassing the hell out of you by taking you right here, and I don't give a damn who's around."

Brandi's eyes widened, because he sounded serious. She scooted to the other side and gave him a dirty look. "I'd care a whole lot, and I hope you remember that. I'm not an exhibitionist."

"That's just depressing." Jazz chuckled from the front seat. "I was hoping."

Desmon laughed with him. "Keep it up and you know Jason is going to kick your ass."

"He could try," Jazz challenged. "Maybe it'll help me work off the frustration."

Jason sighed. "I can't wait for you both to find mates."

"Oh yeah." Brandi agreed. "That *will* be fun. Maybe they'll fall for humans."

"No fucking way. I'm not going through that again." Desmon shook his head. "No offense, Brandi, but that's not in my future."

Jazz didn't say anything. Brandi glanced at his face and she saw such stark grief, it stunned her. She frowned and eyed Jason, seeing that he looked heartsick for his friend. He shook his head and motioned for her to be quiet. It was obvious Jason regretted bringing up the mate issue to begin with.

Somehow what she'd said had made Jazz sad. Maybe he'd fallen for a human and she hadn't been able to accept what he was. Brandi changed the subject instead, asking Jason if he wanted her to move all of her things while they were there or if they were planning a future trip.

Her lease had five more months left on it, but she had never once considered dragging Jason into the human world, even though he offered. He was a god in the woods. He belonged there, and Brandi worked from home. She could do her job anywhere. Forcing him to move would make him miserable, and she loved him too much for that.

Chapter Thirteen

Roni was a petite, curvy brunette with big brown eyes. Her hair was long, hanging clear down to her ass in thick mahogany curls. She wore skin-tight jeans and a low-cut top that showed off impressive cleavage. The beautiful woman shot Jason, Desmon and Jazz a semi-frown, and then she smiled widely at Brandi.

"What in the hell is a pretty girl like you doing hanging out with these mangy mutts?"

"They're kind of cute." Brandi grinned. "They're growing on me."

Roni eyed the three men. She let her gaze run down each of them. "They're okay, but then, I don't really notice all the doggies in town. They aren't my thing."

Desmon chuckled. "Thank God for something. I couldn't handle it if you mated up with one of mine. That'd officially make you one of my problems. Roni, you're too much for anyone to handle, even me, and I'm a professional problem handler."

The brunette grinned and then hugged Desmon like a brother. "Damn straight. I haven't seen you in the bar in a while. You should show your face more."

"I've been busy." Desmon let her go with a grin. "One of these days I'll get a break."

"I hope so. We miss you." Roni turned to Jazz with a glare. "You, on the other hand, need to stay away. I was cleaning up blood for days after the last time with that Goodwin pack wolf you beat the shit out of. It was on the ceiling. True story. I was on a ladder scrubbing it, but I'll forgive you because he grabbed my ass."

Jazz hugged the woman and swatted her ass playfully. "This here is protected land."

Roni turned and showed them her jean-clad ass. "Could you protect it from gravity? Getting old is a bitch."

Jazz laughed. "It looks great to me, but I could find you a mate who'd walk around behind you to hold it up if you're worried."

Desmon snorted. "You think we have anyone that brave in our pack? Jason was the toughest besides us and he's mated now."

"Someone took you on?" Roni spun in shock and grabbed Jason's thick biceps through his shirt. "I've been waiting for this day forever. Who's the bitch? What pack did she flee from?"

Jason gave her a wide, amused smile. "She's not a bitch and she's right here. Brandi's my mate."

The raw shock showed on Roni's face, but she obviously tried to recover before it showed. She slammed her mouth shut and studied Brandi with renewed interest. "Wow, and you decided to stay human?"

Brandi nodded.

"Good for you." Roni grinned. "He looks mean, but we all grew up together. He's a pussycat."

Jason growled, but Roni didn't even flinch. She just lifted her hand and flipped him off. "They don't like cat references, so if he's being a pain in your ass, just buy some yarn, toss it out, and tell him to go play."

Brandi laughed. "He's informed me he doesn't have the urge to chase balls."

"I like you." Roni looped her arm through Brandi's as if they were the best of friends. "Now let's get you de-dog scented and make you smell sweet again."

"I resent that," Jason growled. "And she smells *real* sweet, if you're interested."

Brandi tugged her arm free and closed the distance to Jason. She touched his stomach and tilting her head up to stare into his eyes. "I love your scent. Kiss me bye since we can't touch for a while."

Jason lowered his head and cupped her face with both of his hands. The kiss he planted on her left her panting for air when he slowly released her. His gaze went to Desmon. "Please? Twenty minutes."

"I know it's hard to separate when you're first mated, but no." Desmon shook his head. "We need to get there before dark. We want her noticed, Jason, out in daylight so they're sure it's her. You'll have her back soon enough. I swear."

Jason lowered his gaze. "When I get you alone…"

She nodded and stepped back, making him release her. "I feel the same way."

"I know." He took a long, deep breath, as though savoring it. "You smell good enough to lick for hours, darlin'."

"Enough of that." Roni gripped her arm. "There are some things I'm happier not knowing."

Roni had a nice cabin. The only bathroom was downstairs, and the bath had already been drawn. Roni pointed at Brandi.

"Strip. I have to take these out. We want to make sure your present scent and the new one don't get mixed. You'd be amazed at how well their noses can pick up little things like that."

Brandi tried not to mind getting naked in front of the other woman. Roni didn't look bothered, making it obvious that growing up around Werewolves made her immune to nudity. Then she took Brandi's clothing and left the bathroom. Brandi sank into the hot tub after she was gone, but in minutes, Roni returned wearing shorts and a different top. Her long hair was pulled up in a loose bun on her head.

"I didn't want to contaminate you either." Roni grinned. "I hugged the dog boys out there."

Brandi studied the other woman. "Do you like them or not? You confuse me a little. You act happy to see them, but then you kind of insult them."

"It's a love-hate thing and it's fun to tease them. I'd kill for any of those three boys out there because I know they'd kill for me, but truth be told, I'm not really happy-skippy about the whole wolf thing either. Some of them from the other packs are nightmares. I'm talking worse than any scary movie you've ever seen. Wolves are wolves. They're wild. They're ruled by their instincts more often than not. Even big Des out there in his fancy suits, he's a wolf first, and I've seen what happens to people who forget it, but our pack are good folks, for the most part. It was bad for a while there before Des and Jazz took over, but things have settled now. There are just a few I'd like to see stuffed and mounted in someone's den."

Brandi laughed. "I see."

"So you mated up to a wolf, but you aren't changed? Huh. I've never heard of that one before."

Brandi shrugged. "I don't like the idea of having a tail."

"I don't blame you." Roni grabbed the shampoo. "Turn towards me. I'll wash your hair. My gramps used to wash my hair for me when I was a kid and I loved it. You really need to scrub yourself. Wolf scent is strong, from what I hear. Your being mated to one is tougher, since he's changed your scent from the inside out."

Brandi turned, showing Roni her back and gathering up all her hair so it was easier for Roni to wash. "Thanks for this."

"Don't worry about it. I'm all for taking out assholes. As a matter of fact, I've decided to tag along with you. Not to brag, but I'm impressively talented with guns. Ask anyone. This place is on the Goodwin-Nightwind pack border and sometimes those Goodwin jerks trespass. Let's just say I've had tons of moving targets to shoot at."

"Do they actually try to hurt you?" Brandi asked as Roni squeezed shampoo onto her hair. "Are you in danger here?"

"Nightwind really are good folks for the most part. I wasn't lying about that. A few of 'em have bad habits that carried over from the dark days, but Des and Jazz handle their business. The Goodwin pack, on the other hand, are real bastards. *All of them.* Trust me, you'd never want to meet up with one of those assholes. They don't like humans, have even less respect for women, and they cause trouble wherever they go." Roni started washing Brandi's hair, massaging strong fingers into her skull in way that helped relax some of Brandi's frayed nerves. "You're safe in Hollow Mountain. That's our town. Never go to Hardly or anywhere in that surrounding area. That's Goodwin territory and they'd love to mess with a Nightwind enforcer's mate. It wouldn't be a good time for you, are we clear? They wouldn't dare kill or rape you with Jason's scent all over you, but terrorizing you would be on the table for those creeps."

Brandi turned her head and eyed Roni despite the soap threatening to run into her eyes. "Great. Just what I need, more creepy Werewolves to worry about."

Roni didn't look too concerned as she used a container on the side of the tub and scooped up water. "Tilt your head back, let me rinse it." When Brandi did as told, Roni went on as she poured the warm water over her head, "And don't worry. Jason will protect you. He'll never let something happen to you. Just stick close to home. Everyone's terrified of Jason."

Brandi swallowed. "Why?"

"That man can kick some serious ass. You landed yourself the best fighter in the pack, and he's a great guy to boot. Plus, he's nice to look at. I hate to say it, but watch your back with unmated bitches. They are going to hate that you took him off the market. They come sniffing around a few times a year looking for mates. After Jazz and Des, since they're alphas, your mate is next on their most-wanted list."

Brandi rubbed the water off her forehead and turned to Roni with her mouth hanging open. "Oh my God, I'm never going to survive out here."

"Never fear." Roni grinned. "I know where Jason lives. I've delivered beer and food to his place a few times when he threw parties and had the bar cater them. I'll come out there if you want and teach you how to fire a gun."

"Thanks." Brandi breathed a sigh of relief. "I'd feel better if I knew how to use one."

"Not that I think you'd ever have to fire one for real because Jason is Jason," Roni added. "Most are too afraid of him to even think about messing with someone he loves. The Goodwins are all idiots though, so better safe than sorry. Stay close to home for any shopping trips. Now let's condition your hair and get you dressed."

****

"Thanks for the clothes," Brandi said once she was perfumed and dressed.

"Jason is going to howl when he sees you." Roni had showered and changed too. "You should wear tight clothes more often."

Brandi looked down at herself wearing Roni's skin-tight jeans and low-cut shirt. Roni was thinner than her, which made Brandi think the jeans were an old pair from days when she was bigger. Perhaps Roni even borrowed them from another human friend and was too polite to tell her. That was more likely, because despite what Roni said to the men earlier, there was nothing saggy about her ass.

The other woman had a body to die for, but Brandi wasn't so bothered by it. Jason liked her just as she was, curves and all. It must've been good for her self-esteem. She didn't feel uncomfortable in the clingy clothes and that was a new development. Two weeks ago she wouldn't dare go out of the house in something like this. The lacy push-up bra she wore under the shirt made sure all her best assets were on display and the look worked in a way that was surprising.

Brandi felt sexy.

"He's going to be shocked all right," Brandi agreed as she stared at herself in the mirror over Roni's dresser "I don't own anything even remotely like this."

"Keep everything. I bought them in town this morning and just wore them for an hour before you arrived, so they'd have my scent on them like they wanted. Des paid for them, so they're yours. Let's go." Roni walked over to a chair by the door. There was a duffle bag there that Roni tossed over her shoulder. "After you — and don't go near them."

That explained the jeans, and it meant Desmon probably went into great detail describing her because they fit surprisingly well. Usually, Brandi would die of embarrassment, but with the wolves, it wasn't such a big thing that she wasn't bone thin. She got the impression Jason wasn't the only one who liked women with meat on their bones.

Brandi walked outside and spotted Desmon, Jazz, and Jason leaning against the SUV talking. Jason's head snapped in her direction and his nose flared, as though he was trying to smell her. Brandi grinned and put her hands on her hips. Then she slowly turned. When she fully made a circle so Jason could take in her new look, she saw Jazz and Desmon gripping Jason's arms as if they were barely holding him back.

Jason growled, a low, dangerous wolf growl that made Brandi tingle in all the right places.

"Looking too good," Jazz called out. "Couldn't you have bought her something baggy and hideous, Roni?"

"Nope," Roni said with a broad smile. "What's wrong, Jason? See something you like? Did you notice that your mate's got big boobs? Don't they look nice all pushed up and getting some sunshine?"

"Yeah, *baby*." Jazz laughed as he eyed Jason. "Give you any ideas?"

Jason snarled and tried to break out of the alphas' hold. He didn't get far, and his gaze locked on Brandi. "If you like that bra, you better take it off before I'm allowed to touch you."

She laughed. "Thanks for the warning this time. I'd like to have at least one bra that isn't torn up."

"I'm coming. Don't argue," Roni yelled from behind her. "I'm locked and loaded for a fight and I can go in with her in case someone slips past you."

Desmon just nodded. "Thanks, Roni."

"Yeah, thanks." Jason took another long, cooling breath. "That makes me feel better."

Roni held up a hand to the men, and then led Brandi to her black truck. She tossed the duffle bag in the back and then both of them climbed in. Roni drove. They listened to the radio mostly, and exchanged some girl talk, which was nice after being surrounded by nothing but men for almost a week. The drive was long, but Roni drove faster than the speed limit. Desmon's SUV was behind them and Roni pointed out a pair of motorcycles also following. She told Brandi they were pack.

When they finally got to her place, Roni parked and Desmon pulled around the street rather than follow her into the parking garage. The guys on the motorcycles went in the opposite direction, and something about being so far from Jason made Brandi's chest hurt.

She felt lonely, even knowing he was just around the corner, and she was glad she had Roni with her.

When they got to her apartment, Brandi unlocked the door and led Roni inside. Roni dropped her duffle bag on the floor, and then whistled as she looked around. "Whoa, nice place."

Brandi shrugged. "I saved and bought each piece. It's been a work in progress."

"I'm scared to touch anything." Roni looked at the entryway table in the foyer. "Jason obviously hasn't been to your place, has he?"

Brandi shook her head. "No, why?"

Roni turned and faced Brandi, looking uncertain all of a sudden. "You're high class. Have you met Jason or seen his place? He's basics to the fullest."

Brandi glanced around her apartment. She had pristine white carpet. Her couches were Victorian. Her coffee table and end table were replicas of eighteenth-century Chippendales. She had a few tapestries on the walls, but they were replicas too. She couldn't afford the real things. Those could run into the hundreds of thousands of dollars depending on their condition.

"What is it you do for a living?" Roni was still eyeing her hesitantly.

"I'm a self-employed accountant."

Roni just arched an eyebrow at Brandi. "I see."

Brandi frowned. "What?"

"Does Jason know you make good money?"

"Not really that good. I only cleared eighty thousand last year. I just live alone and have minimal expenses."

Roni let out a snort of disbelief. "I made thirty-two last year. Jason probably doesn't make much more. He's pack paid. Hollow Mountain doesn't have any big companies."

Brandi looked around her apartment again. "I like Jason's cabin better. None of this matters, and he told me he'd like me to stay home and have kids. I could do that and cut my hours down to part time. I always wanted to have kids. Being a stay-at-home mom sounds wonderful."

"I guess." Roni shrugged. "Just as long as you're happy. So relax. I'll guard the door."

"I have some calls to make. I need to cancel the six credit cards in my wallet and handle some other banking stuff. I don't like that my purse was unattended for all that time. Luckily, I don't carry checks, and I have fraud protection either way. I should've done it at Jason's, but he kept distracting me."

"Six!" Roni gasped. "You have six credit cards? Geez, girl, how much debt are you in? Maybe you should tell Jason you just put him in the poor house."

"I carry zero balances. Every month I pay them off."

"Wow, it's nice to be you." Roni shook her head. "If I had six credit cards, I'd be in debt up to my eyebrows."

Brandi snorted with amusement and walked to her bedroom. She eyed her room. It was Victorian too, done in pinks and white. Very girly. She knew without a doubt that Jason would hate it. She walked to her desk, pulled her laptop out of the bag she brought with her, and started making calls. In minutes, she was caught up in contacting her credit card companies and her bank. She also placed a call to the apartment manager and asked the woman to have her locks changed immediately.

Brandi's cell beeped while she sat on hold. She hung up on the credit card company without hesitating when she saw it was Jason. "Are you okay?"

"Hi, darlin'. What are you doing in there? Are you naked?"

"Not likely with Roni here."

Jason laughed. "I wanted to tell you heads-up. Company pulled in at the back of the building. Lock your doors and keep your head down."

He hung up before she could respond.

Brandi's heart pounded. She sat there stunned for a moment when she realized this was really happening, then she ran out of her room. Roni was gripping a shotgun. A handgun sat on the entry hall table as she stood by the door, squinting out the peephole.

"That was Jason. He said we have company in the back and to lock everything down. We're supposed to keep our heads down."

"Des called me too." Roni nodded. "Go lock yourself in the bathroom. It's not near any exterior walls. Huddle in the tub. If bullets fly, that's where you'll be safest."

"What about my neighbors?"

"I doubt a bullet will ever be fired. Wolves like to keep things physical with hand-to-claw combat."

"Shit." Brandi sighed, knowing she couldn't leave this woman to fight her battles for her. "Do you need help? Do you want me to hold the gun? It's point and fire, right?"

Roni chuckled. "If anyone gets to this door past your mate, I'd be shocked. I'm just here because I was bored. I wasn't working today. Go in the bathroom. Maybe you can pack up some of your stuff while you're in there. I have a feeling Jason is going to see this place and want to leave fast. It kind of reminds me of a museum."

Chapter Fourteen

Since the moment Roni's black truck pulled into the parking garage, Jason's entire body had been tense. He was wound so tight, he jerked and growled at Jazz when the alpha touched Jason's shoulder to point out two white vans pulling into the lot behind Brandi's building.

Jazz held up his hands at Jason's show of aggression, for once not teasing as he said, "Relax. I get it, okay? We'll get this done and you'll be back with her."

Jason nodded, thinking of Jazz and his situation. Before now he'd never fully understood what it was like for Jazz to lose his perspective mate as a teenager. Jazz hid the pain with humor, but the wolves in their pack all knew he had never recovered.

Brandi had changed Jason. Now he truly knew what it was like to have a woman he would do anything for. Even if their relationship was still new, Jason would tear down entire empires to protect his mate without thinking. The fact that she was human made it so much more difficult. It physically hurt knowing how vulnerable she was to the anger of wolves.

To lose her…

Jason shuddered, hoping he never knew that loss like Jazz did. He couldn't even comprehend a pain like that.

"Hey, don't worry, big wolf, we'll make sure she's safe." Jazz reached back from his seat next to Desmon and grabbed his shoulder reassuringly. "I promise. You're not losing your mate, Jason."

"We got your back," Desmon added as he turned around from the driver's seat and gave him a hard look. "We're taking these bastards down. Call Brandi, give her a heads-up, and then let's do this."

"Keep it light," Jazz warned. "Don't be growling at her and scaring her for no reason."

So, Jason called Brandi. He kept it light like Jazz suggested, but his body was still coiled tight as he watched the other wolves get out of the vans. They weren't well-kept wolves, like the ones in his pack. Their clothes were ragged, and they were all lean, with scraggly hair. It didn't make Jason feel better.

"These are some feral wolves," Desmon warned Roni, who he'd called at the same time Jason reached out to Brandi. "Stay on guard."

Jason went ahead and hung up with Brandi in case she could hear the background conversation. These wolves barely looked human, and they were in the city. Some Weres lost complete touch of their humanity, choosing instead to fully embrace their animalistic sides. The results were terrifying, not just for humans but for Weres too.

Packs this blatantly obvious risked exposing them all.

Jason grabbed the door handle, but Jazz reached out to stop him once more. "Hold on."

Jason growled, low and dangerous. "They're heading for her building."

He could smell the wolves, their scent filthy, deadly and primal. Jason didn't want them anywhere near Brandi. It was going to take extreme restraint to capture rather than kill.

"Look." Desmon tilted his head towards the parking lot. "Bad timing."

A police car had pulled up next to one of the vans. They couldn't very well attack five rabid Weres in front of a human police officer.

"Call Miles," Desmon said to Jazz. "Make sure they hold off until we can see what this cop's doing."

"Sure," Jazz said, and then sniffed as the car door to the police vehicle opened. A middle-aged man got out, dressed in simple jeans and a t-shirt instead of a uniform, but that wasn't what was most noticeable. "Christ, that cologne that cop's wearing. He reeks. There's no way human women like that."

"They do, though." Desmon shrugged. "Go to a human bar sometime. All the men smell like that and they're getting dates."

Jason watched the five wolves stalk towards the back of the building in typical pack formation. He growled again. "Fuck the cop; we're letting them get to her."

"We won't let them hurt her," Desmon said calmly to Jason while Jazz made the phone call to the other pack members waiting in the front. "We can't risk exposing ourselves to human law enforcement." He turned back to Jazz. "Did they disable all the cameras on the building?"

"Yes," Jazz said in exasperation, though he was still on the phone with Miles. "We've told you that at least five times."

Desmon didn't look apologetic. "You're irritated now, but if they missed one—"

"They didn't." Jazz groaned. "I hate the city. It makes everything complicated. How do those city packs handle jumping through all these hoops?"

"Who knows," Desmon said, as if it was foreign to him too, as they watched the door.

Jason didn't know how they stayed so casual, but he also understood the alphas had good reason for their relaxed confidence. There were seven wolves from Nightwind here to protect Brandi. Now they knew only five wolves from the other pack had shown up to attack her. The odds were in their favor this time, when it had been the two alphas against the world since they were teenagers.

"The cop's going to the front," Jazz said into the phone. "Move around to the back, we're right behind you."

Jason didn't hesitate. He opened the door and jumped out. He'd waited long enough and he'd be damned if he was trusting his mate's safety to other wolves. He yanked his shirt over his head and tossed it in the SUV.

"Fuck!" Jazz cursed.

Desmon opened the driver's-side door and jumped out.

"Don't shift," Desmon warned, his voice low and gravelly with alpha authority. "You better not fucking shift in the city, Jason!"

Jason wasn't real sure how he was going to manage that when he was feeling so animalistic. He could only hope his wolf would listen to his alpha, even if everything in him was opposed to it. When it came down to a war between protecting his mate and obeying Desmon, Jason wasn't so sure things would turn out how his alpha wanted.

Jason was halfway across the lot when something made him stop. He sniffed, still catching the scent of the police officer's cologne. Something smelled off, but he couldn't quite place it.

On instinct, he looked to Desmon, who stopped too and looked behind him with a frown on his face.

Jazz voiced it for both of them. "The fucking cop."

It slammed into Jason then—the scent of wolf masked in cologne. He changed gears, knowing that Miles and the other enforcers were already taking care of the enemy pack members who'd walked to the back.

Jason ran to the front entrance at full speed, hoping to God this wolf didn't have enough time to get to Brandi.

He burst into the doors and took another deep breath. The cologne made the cop easy to track, and Jason knew he'd taken the elevator. It had barely dinged closed when he got in there, and Jason knew the other wolf likely smelled him too.

Desmon stormed in. "Take the stairs."

"I don't know what floor she's on," Jason confessed as he opened the emergency staircase, thinking it was incredibly stupid that he hadn't asked Brandi before she took off with Roni.

"I got you." Desmon came up behind him, making it obvious he knew because of his earlier reconnaissance on her building. "She's on the fourth floor."

They took the stairs two at a time, running so fast that if there were still cameras, they would easily record that neither of them were fully human. Desmon grabbed the handle when they hit the fourth floor. Even before he'd fully opened it, a low warning growl greeted them.

Desmon growled back, sounding very much like an alpha wolf who was used to warning enemies of his power before attacking.

Jason just punched the older wolf with a blind fury, acting like an enforcer instead of an alpha wolf. He could smell Brandi now, her sweet scent calling to the wolf in him, and knowing an enemy had gotten this close to hurting her shattered Jason's control. If the other wolf hadn't heard them coming up the stairs, he would've gotten to her.

Fuck Desmon's orders.

Jason was going to kill this wolf, and he likely said it as he jumped at him, forcing the bastard to the carpeted floor before he could recover from Jason's first punch. Then Jason slammed his fist into his face again, this time twice as hard, feeling a keen satisfaction when he felt a nose break under his knuckles.

Jason didn't shift like he wanted to. It turned out Desmon's authority was respected enough by Jason's wolf that he stayed in skin—barely. He did, however, beat the fuck out of this other wolf. For the most part, Desmon just stood there and let him, as if he understood Jason needed the outlet.

"Jason, he's out!" Desmon finally snapped at him. "You can't kill this wolf in the hallway of your mate's apartment building. You're getting blood all over the carpet. STOP!"

When Jason punched the other wolf again, Desmon physically pulled Jason off him. Desmon just threw Jason against the wall as if he was some teenage wolf having a temper tantrum, and it was way too easy for the alpha. It sort of freaked Jason out, because he hadn't been in a fight with Desmon since they were pups and even then they were playful. Jason had almost forgotten how massively powerful Desmon was in a fight, but he shouldn't have. Desmon had been one of the wolves who helped Jason grow stronger when they were young, because in a way he understood Jason. Though Desmon's mother had been changed long before she got pregnant with him, considering she'd been in a love match with his father, she was born human—just like Jason's father.

Desmon was full wolf, but he had a soft spot a mile wild for humans.

He'd even loved one once, but that ended almost as badly as Jazz's story had. It was part of the reason why Jason had avoided humans. Now the alpha wolf had no interest in a mate, especially not a human one, but he still championed humans in a way most wolves didn't. It hadn't always been that way in their pack. Growing up, the old alpha of their pack had been vicious, and he'd held a deep-seated hatred for humans. It made Jason's childhood particularly brutal, but he knew it would've been a lot worse without Desmon and Jazz there to help make him strong.

Desmon narrowed light eyes at him and growled, "I said stop."

Jason took a deep breath, trying and failing to get his raging emotions under control. In the end, even if he was still in skin, Jason was more wolf than anything when he apologized. "Sorry, Alpha."

"It's okay." Desmon sighed and let go of Jason. Then he squeezed his shoulder reassuringly. "I understand more than I want to."

"Do you?" Jason asked curiously, his wolf still right on the surface and desperate for some understanding. "Do you still miss her? Like Jazz misses his human? You understand how much it scares me knowing she's so vulnerable?"

Desmon's features grew tense all of a sudden, and Jason realized he had stepped in it. Jazz's human was killed, but Desmon's had run away from him. That was a decidedly different set of circumstances.

Jason might have apologized, but the man on the ground suddenly sprang to his feet and took off down the hallway. He was shockingly fast, especially considering Jason had nearly killed him—or so he'd thought.

"What the hell?" Desmon sounded stunned too.

The guy was cornered at the end of the hallway with no stairs, and no time to wait for the elevator. Jason wasn't real sure what this other wolf thought he was going to do when he was facing both of them. Desmon may be letting Jason fight his own battles, but that didn't mean he'd let this guy get away—no matter how fast he thought he was.

Then the other wolf kicked in an apartment door and disappeared inside.

Jason and Desmon barreled after him. Thank God there were no humans home in the apartment. The other wolf was at a window, and in one swift kick, he used his Were strength to break the frame, knocking the window out and sending shattered glass to the pavement below. Jason and Desmon both leapt for him then when they realized what he was going to do, but they were too late.

He jumped.

The two of them went to the open window, the wind hitting their faces as they watched the injured wolf shake off the jump and run for a small woodsy park behind the building.

"This motherfucker's crazy," Desmon whispered in awe. "Jazz'll have to —"

Jason didn't hear the rest of what he said, because he jumped after him. If that wolf could survive a four-story jump, Jason knew he could it too.

He landed on his feet, but it wasn't easy. He had no idea how cat shifters did this shit on a regular basis. It felt like he'd shattered every bone in his body, but somehow he still remained standing.

His legs hurt, but he took off towards the park.

He could see the man in front of him, running and pulling off his shirt, making it obvious he was intent on shifting, but Jason already had a head start in that regard. Jason's shirt was still in Desmon's SUV. The wolf under his skin was anxious to break free, and Jason pulled at the button to his jeans, knowing if they were undone they'd be easier to shake off once he was in fur.

Unfortunately, he never got a chance to tear into this bastard with teeth.

Desmon came out of nowhere and tackled the other wolf just as Jason was gaining on him.

Jason watched as both of them fell to the grass, growling viciously. Neither fully shifted, but they were both halfway there, with hair growing on their faces and arms. Desmon's teeth were long and vicious as he snarled, "I should let him kill you for that! It was four stories! Do I look like a goddamn panther?"

The other wolf just laughed. His face was bloody and dirty, but his green eyes were glazed and manic, as if Desmon's misery was worth it all. "I was going to eat her myself, you know. I wasn't even going to share her with the others," he confessed, his voice low with the wolf in him. He turned his head and looked at Jason. "You ever taste human? I guess you have. I heard him say you mated her."

Jason growled and stepped forward threateningly.

"Does she taste good? Your juicy little mate?"

Jason flashed his teeth at the prone wolf still struggling under Desmon's massive strength. Jason was partially shifted too, and if a human found them like that, they'd surely run screaming from this little patch of manufactured green space in the city.

"Jazz, shut this fucker up!" Desmon called out before Jason could respond.

Jason turned to see Jazz looking no worse for the wear as he ran up behind them.

"We'll let you kill him," Jazz promised, finally pacifying the wolf in Jason. Then Jazz pulled a strip of duct tape off the roll in his hand as though it was his official job. He bit the edge of the tape with his teeth that he let grow long, and tore it free from the roll. "I'll even let you drag it out a little—or a lot."

Desmon had one hand in the other wolf's hair, using his hold to wrench his head back painfully. His other hand was wrapped around the guy's throat so tightly he was starting to turn blue, but he certainly wasn't talking anymore.

Desmon didn't let him breathe again until Jazz taped his mouth. Then together the two alphas struggled to bind the wolf's hands behind his back.

"He's feisty for an older wolf," Jazz observed as he wrapped the tape over and over again around the wolf's wrists. "He's got to be at least three hundred."

"He's the alpha," Jason said as Desmon finally sat the other wolf up. Their enemy was silent now, huffing and puffing under the tape like he was still trying to catch his breath. Jazz had wrapped more tape around his head, making sure he couldn't spew any more of his brutal bullshit, no matter how hard he tried. Still, he fought against the bindings on his wrists as Jason studied him coldly, remembering Brandi's description. "This is him. She said their alpha had green eyes and scars like that."

"Probably is," Jazz agreed. "Is it too soon to talk about how sick that jump was?"

"Way too soon," Desmon huffed as he got to his feet and dragged the other wolf with him.

"I saw the whole thing," Jazz went on as if he hadn't heard Desmon. "When this motherfucker took it, I thought maybe my nose is wrong. Maybe he's half tiger or something, but then Jason did it—which was very badass, by the way."

"Thanks," Jason grunted. "It didn't feel badass. My legs still hurt."

"And I'm thinking, there's no fucking way Des will do it, 'cause we know you and heights, but then—"

"What the fuck were you doing while we were jumping out of windows?" Desmon cut him off, his voice still low and furious.

"Damage control. The guys had those other wolves easily. All they did was let Miles work off some of his anger issues. Maybe he'll be in a decent mood for fifteen minutes."

Desmon took a deep breath, as if it made sense. It was essentially what he'd been doing upstairs until this wolf went nuts. Before then, he'd let Jason work off some of his anger.

"They're loading the other ones in their vans," Jazz explained when they walked back into the parking lot. "I figure Miles and Luke can drive the vans back to our territory. Jason can take Brandi home in your SUV and we'll take the bikes back. We'll just leave the cop car here, 'cause I crawled in and sniffed around. That thing is not his. He stole it. At least we hope he only stole it. I didn't smell blood, so hopefully that's all it was and he didn't attack the cop it belonged to. Either way, I figure you could use the ride."

"I'm okay." Desmon took a deep breath. "If this is the alpha, then our problem's solved. Maybe I'll get to sleep for once. Let's get Brandi down here to identify him and get the hell out of here before the humans start missing that cop car. Don't say anything to her about suspecting this one, Jason. Don't give her details. Sometimes trauma can make a person's memory foggy. Don't plant ideas in her head. So just let her look and decide."

"I don't even want her to see him," Jason growled.

"It'll be quick." Desmon smiled as if he wasn't dragging a very reluctant, beaten, and duct-taped wolf along with him. "Then it'll be over and you two can have your mating honeymoon."

Jason looked to Jazz. "And you'll let me kill him, right? You promised."

"Hell yes," Jazz assured him. "I'm an alpha of my word and even if I wasn't, I heard what this bastard said to you. Sick fuck."

Jason nodded in agreement. "Then okay, I don't want her to hear the details anyway. I don't want her to know how close he got to her. Let's just get it over with."

Chapter Fifteen

Brandi packed up her bathroom in a few overnight cases to fight the anxiousness. She walked into her bedroom next and found the luggage set she had stored under her canopy bed. She started loading up her favorite clothes, her pictures, and everything that had sentimental value to her. She studied the room again, knowing none of her furniture would look good in Jason's house. She'd have to donate it to charity. Someone would get lucky; maybe one of the women in the pack wanted it. It didn't look like Roni's style, or she'd offer it to her.

Brandi's cell phone on the desk rang and she nearly tripped in her urgency to grab the phone. She answered it quickly. "Are you okay?"

"Yeah." Jason was out of breath. "Come out back, darlin'. We have six of these bastards. I want you to take a look at them."

Brandi noticed it was dark outside when she walked back into the living room. Roni had set her shotgun down and instead shoved the handgun in the front of her jeans. She tugged her shirt over it and led the way. Brandi followed her down the stairs and through the complex. The back was all carports and open parking. She spotted two white vans. Jason was standing by one, and he waved them over.

Jason's shirt was torn. He had a scratch on his forehead, but he smiled at her and she couldn't help but grin back. Jason waited until she got close before he gripped the side sliding door to jerk it open.

Inside were three men. They were tied up tight, bleeding and bruised. Jazz was sitting in the passenger seat with a gun, looking very mean and alpha-like, but he winked at Brandi.

Brandi studied the three men, feeling her heart sink as she looked back to Jason.

"He's not here."

Jason nodded. "Let's try the other group then."

Brandi followed Jason to the second van. A man she didn't know was guarding that door. He grabbed the handle and Jason put his arm around her waist as the other pack member pulled the door open. She chewed on her lip and looked at the three Werewolves, bound and beaten bloody.

The light wasn't the greatest in the van, but her eyes locked on one man.

"That's him."

"I knew it." Jason growled at the alpha wolf. "You're dead. No one's saving you this time."

The man snarled under the duct-tape wound around his face. Cold, watery green eyes glared at Brandi, but she stared back at him rather than flinch away.

"I guess I'm the one who gets the last laugh now, huh, asshole? Only you can't run for your life, can you?" she snapped at the vicious alpha wolf, knowing it was Jason giving her the strength to do it. She wrapped her arms around Jason's waist, and turned away from the van, wanting to forget those cold, terrifying green eyes. "So it's over?"

Jason pulled her tighter into his arms. "The guys are going to drive these assholes to our territory. We'll figure out who the hell they are, and then yeah, it's going to be over." Jason turned and snarled at the older man, showing deadly canine teeth that had grown long. "I'll remove his damn head myself."

The guy holding the van door slid it shut. Then he climbed into the driver's seat and Brandi stood there shaking as the van backed away. Jazz jumped out of the other van while two more pack members climbed in, and the second van drove away too.

Desmon walked up; his T-shirt was torn too and his jeans were as filthy. It was clear he wasn't the sort of boss to sit back and let others do the dirty work.

The tall, handsome alpha wolf held out his hands as though catching that many rogue Werewolves was all in a day's work. "Mission accomplished."

"Thank you," Brandi said softly to Desmon.

"No, thank *you*." Desmon chuckled. "You were the live bait."

Jason kissed her forehead. "I didn't forget about getting you alone. Let's grab some of your shit and get home. I have plans."

"Yeah. Let's all go up to Brandi's." Roni laughed as Jazz walked up to them. "I can't wait for you to see her place."

Jason nodded, and draped his arm over her shoulder, clearly determined to keep her close. Brandi glanced up at him and felt nervous as they walked back to her building. She hoped he didn't have the reaction that Roni had.

Roni took the lead as they headed upstairs and Brandi found herself almost dragging her feet. It turned out her nervousness wasn't misplaced.

When Jason walked in the door, he halted as if he'd run into an invisible wall. Brandi watched his eyes widen as he took in her apartment. Then he turned back to her, staring at Brandi as if he didn't recognize her.

She smiled, hiding her apprehension, hoping he couldn't smell it. "I packed my things already. It's all on my bed. The rest I'll donate to charity."

Jason blinked, and looked physically pale like she'd never seen before. Strange that he could fight deadly Werewolves with no problem, but her apartment shook him up so noticeably. Jazz and Desmon were silent and unusually still, making it obvious they were surprised too.

Jason tore his gaze from hers to look around the apartment again. Then he released her hand and walked into the bedroom.

"Help out, guys." Jason's voice was barely human. "She's a woman. They pack a lot of shit."

Jazz and Desmon followed him into her bedroom, both of them still quiet.

Roni sighed softly once they were alone. "Not good."

"Why is he so upset?" Brandi asked, even if she knew the men could probably hear.

Roni gave her a sympathetic smile, and whispered when she spoke. "He'll get over it. They are *really* proud. It's a wolf thing, and you have nicer shit. He found you with nothing in the woods. He provided everything for you. Now he walks into this. He just got a reality bitch-slap."

Brandi moved fast for the bedroom door.

Jazz and Desmon were watching Jason with scowls on their handsome faces. Jason was at her dresser, with her jewelry box open. He lifted her grandmother's diamond tennis bracelet. He dropped it and picked up a few of her diamond rings before he softly growled.

"Jason?" Her voice was shaky.

He turned, and the look in his eyes almost scared her. He seemed confused, maybe even hurt, and she went to him on instinct

"I'm not taking that." She closed the lid to her jewelry box. "My stuff's on the bed."

He frowned at her. "You didn't tell me you came from this."

"From what? A museum?" She used Roni's word, thinking for the first time how much it fit. Her old life seemed so cold now that she had Jason. "None of this matters, but you want to know what does? You've given me the things I've always wanted. A real home. Happiness." She moved closer, until they were touching. "Love. Great sex. You make me like myself. I feel daring and sexy when I'm with you. You make me naughty in a way I never thought I'd have the chance to be." She grinned at that one. "You make me feel alive. The knowledge that every night, when you hold me in your arms, I'm in the one place in the world that I want to be most...that's what matters to me." She hugged him because she couldn't resist. "You give me yourself, Jason."

He reached down and brushed her face with the back of his knuckles before he slowly smiled. "Are you really giving it to charity? I hate this shit, but I'd sleep in a pink and white bed if you were in it. I'd feel less sexy, but I'd do it."

Relief and happiness filled Brandi. "It's so gone. I love your bed much more. It's got great springs. It's got better memories too."

He chuckled before he eyed her bed again. "We could give yours a try."

"Are you kidding?" She gave him a look of horror. "That old thing? It would snap apart the second we got undressed."

Jason planted a kiss on her that left her breathless. "Your jewelry box comes. My mother would have killed for any of this shit. You're a woman. I bet some of it is from your family.

My mom had a few nice rings from her family that were passed down. She said girls do that."

She nodded. "They do."

Jason turned and lifted the jewelry box. He gently handed it over to her. "You carry that. We'll get the bags."

She smiled and walked out of the room. Roni was standing there, trying to look casual, but she winked conspiratorially.

"Good save," Roni whispered when she walked up to Brandi. "I'm impressed."

"I meant every word," Brandi told her solemnly. "This place feels so lifeless to me now. I bought possessions to fill the hole in my life. It's all I had. None of this stuff ever made me happy, but Jason does."

Roni's smile widened. "You're definitely the right woman to be Jason's mate."

Chapter Sixteen

Jason and Brandi made love frantically once they got back to the cabin. Then Jason left early the next morning, and she'd known where he was going. He wanted to be present when Desmon and Jazz interrogated the six men who'd been captured stalking her apartment building, to say nothing of the alpha who'd had her kidnapped and almost killed.

The nightmare was actually over.

Jason showered when he came home and Brandi had breakfast waiting for him when he walked back downstairs. She sat across from him as he ate, but she wanted to wait until he was done before they talked about anything unpleasant. Unable to resist, she went to him and sat on his lap when he pushed away from the table. Brandi smiled as he hugged her closer to him, and then rested her head against his chest.

"How did it go?" she finally asked.

"Good." He rubbed her arm soothingly as he said it. "It was a small outfit. They were looking for a new territory after a company came in and built condos on the little running land they had in the city. They heard we were a small pack. Which we actually are, but then again, we have two alpha best friends who run our pack. It's always been an ace up our sleeve. Most packs only have one alpha to defend their pack. They were planning on using you to get our attention. He probably thought it would scare us off." Jason shook his head. "We don't scare off, and it's too bad for them they didn't get the memo, because their territory problems are solved now. Permanently. They'll never be bothering us again. We found them a new home in hell."

Brandi was quiet for a moment as she considered his words. She wasn't the least bit bothered that the man responsible for almost killing her was dead, but he wasn't the only one. They were all gone now. Maybe his pack members didn't deserve to die with him, but if the others she met were anything to go by, they probably did.

Something about Jason's wolf mentality was rubbing off on her. It seemed fair in the world of kill or be killed these Werewolves live in. The Nightwinds had just been minding their own business and this pack attacked them.

That was their mistake.

Brandi tilted her head and smiled up at him. "I can't see anything making you run away in fear."

"You've never seen me in the mall. I hate those places. Too many people. Too many smells. It's not natural to have that many damn stores in one place. I run to the nearest exit to get the hell out every time I try. I don't last ten minutes in those places."

"Malls?" She laughed. "Really?"

"Says the woman who screamed about a tiny spider in the shower stall the other morning."

"It looked mean," she said without apology. "They have eight legs. *Eight.* That's not right."

"It was a baby."

"Babies have mothers. If the baby was that scary, imagine how terrifying the mother is."

"If you say so." Jason wrapped his arms tighter around her and admitted, "You make me happier than I've ever been in my life."

"Same to you," she said softly. "I love you, Jason."

"I know." He grinned, looking unabashedly pleased. "I love you too, darlin'."

Her smile grew broader, and she knew the uncontained happiness showed. "I know."

Then Brandi gasped when Jason gripped her hips and lifted her. She heard his dishes hit the floor and he suddenly had her pinned on top of the table. "I'm still hungry."

"Really?"

Jason nodded as he reached for her skirt, shoving it up. When he smiled, his canine teeth were long as he confessed, "Starving."

"What big teeth you have," she said with a false look of horror.

"The better to eat you with," he promised as he pulled at her panties, sliding them down her thighs. "How does that sound?"

"Sounds fair to me, but maybe later," Brandi decided as she reached for the front of his jeans. "I have a real craving for something myself."

Jason growled at her, and a shudder of pleasure washed over Brandi. The sounds he made always turned her on in the worst way, and it was obvious he could smell it. He tossed her panties towards the sink and pushed her thighs wider apart as he closed his eyes to breathe her in with another low growl.

"I'd tear yours off, but you don't wear any." Brandi laughed as she unzipped his jeans and shoved them down.

"I wish you didn't." Jason's voice was still raspy and primal. "We're in the woods now, darlin'. You don't need those things."

She smiled. "I could be tempted to toss them all in the trash."

He arched an eyebrow at her. "Really? And what would I have to do or say to get you to do that?"

She pulled him down on top of her in response. He followed her lead easily, pinning her under him, making it obvious that was exactly where he wanted to be. She loved his weight on her, and she wrapped her arms around his neck to keep him there.

Then she leaned up and kissed him, before she whispered against his lips, "I want you."

Jason kissed her back. "You got me, darlin'."

"Then there goes the underwear. Consider them all in the trash." She wrapped her legs around his waist. "I want you right now."

Jason entered her, and Brandi moaned his name at the feel of his thick, hard cock stretching her, setting off every pleasure sensor she had. She tightened her legs around his hips, clinging to him, desperate for the hard, driving need to take over. Jason pushed into her deep, but then he stopped. She opened her eyes, giving him a look of silent protest.

"Tell me you love me again," he demanded. "Let me hear it."

"Now?"

"Tell me."

"I love you," she promised him. "You're everything to me."

"You've really made me the happiest I've ever been in my life." He brushed his mouth over hers. "I love you, Brandi. You have no idea how much I love you."

"But I would have an idea if you decided to start moving again." She shifted under him to make her point. "You could show me, you know, because I'm not feeling the love when you hold still like that."

He softly growled. "Hang on to me, darlin', 'cause I got a hell of a lot of love for you, and I'm going to spend the rest of our lives showing you how much."

"So, shut up already and prove it."

"Consider it done," Jason chuckled as he leaned down and kissed her again.

THE END

TITLES BY LAURAN DOHNER

NEW SPECIES

Fury (New Species Book 1)

Slade (New Species Book 2)

Valiant (New Species Book 3)

Justice (New Species Book 4)

Brawn (New Species Book 5)

Wrath (New Species Book 6)

Tiger (New Species Book 7)

Obsidian (New Species Book 8)

Shadow (New Species Book 9)

Moon (New Species Book 10)

True (New Species Book 11)

Darkness (New Species Book 12)

Smiley (New Species Book 13)

Numbers (New Species Book 14)

CYBORG SEDUCTION

Burning Up Flint (Cyborg Seduction Book 1)

Kissing Steel (Cyborg Seduction Book 2)

Melting Iron (Cyborg Seduction Book 3)

Touching Ice (Cyborg Seduction Book 4)

Stealing Coal (Cyborg Seduction Book 5)

Redeeming Zorus (Cyborg Seduction Book 6)

Taunting Krell (Cyborg Seduction Book 7)

Haunting Blackie (Cyborg Seduction Book 8)

Loving Deviant (Cyborg Seduction Book 9)

Seducing Stag (Cyborg Seduction Book 10)

VLG

Drantos (VLG Series Book 1)

Kraven (VLG Series Book 2)

Lorn (VLG Book 3)

ZORN WORRIORS

Ral's Woman (Zorn Warriors Book 1)

Kidnapping Casey (Zorn Warriors Book 2)

Tempting Rever (Zorn Warriors Book 3)

Berrr's Vow (Zorn Warriors Book 4)

MATING HEAT

Mate Set (Mating Heat Book 1)

His Purrfect Mate (Mating Heat Book 2)

Mating Brand (Mating Heat Book 3)

RIDING THE RAINES

Propositioning Mr. Raine (Riding the Raines Book 1)

Raine on Me (Riding the Raines Book 2)

Claws And Fangs

TITLES BY KELE MOON

* * * *

BATTERED HEARTS Series M/F

Defying the Odds

Star Crossed

Crossing the Line

UNTAMED HEARTS Series *M/F*

The Viper

The Slayer

The Enforcer

EDEN Series

Beyond Eden M/M/F

Finding Eden M/M

Claiming Eden M/M

STANDALONE NOVELS

The Queens Consorts M/M/F

Starfish and Coffee M/M

Packing Heat M/M

SHORTS

A Kiss for Luck M/F

Mercy Bound M/F